VALERIE'S RUSSIA

1913: An unexpected offer from the Empress of Russia, who seeks an English companion for her children, brings Valerie Marsh to the Alexander Palace at Tsarskoe Selo. There, she is torn between two cultures — and two passions: Pyotr Silakov, a handsome young cavalry officer in the Tsar's household; and Grigorii Rasputin, the Tsarina's holy man and friend. But Silakov, obliged to marry the rich and beautiful Sophia Lukaev, wants Valerie only for his mistress; whilst folk whisper that Rasputin is nothing but a lecherous charlatan . . . Meanwhile, the clouds of war loom on the horizon — what will become of Valerie when the storm breaks?

Books by Sara Judge
Published by Ulverscroft:

THE GYPSY'S RETURN
LUCIFER'S HOLD
TUDOR STAR
THE BLOODSTONE RING
THE ORANGE MISTRESS
TABATHA'S REVENGE
QUEST FOR A LORD
HONEY BROWN IS MARRIED

SARA JUDGE

◆

VALERIE'S RUSSIA

Complete and Unabridged

ULVERSCROFT
Leicester

First published in Great Britain in 2014 by
Robert Hale Limited
London

First Large Print Edition
published 2015
by arrangement with
Robert Hale Limited
London

A catalogue record for this book is available
from the British Library.

ISBN 978–1–4448–2471–1

Published by
F. A. Thorpe (Publishing)
Anstey, Leicestershire

Set by Words & Graphics Ltd.
Anstey, Leicestershire
Printed and bound in Great Britain by
T. J. International Ltd., Padstow, Cornwall

This book is printed on acid-free paper

For Sarah

1

Autumn 1913 – Tsarskoe Selo

Valerie Marsh was met at Tsarskoe Selo railway station by a tall cavalry officer.

'Pyotr Silakov,' he introduced himself, bowing smartly then jerking his head at the man-servant to take Valerie's two suitcases.

'The motor car awaits us in the yard, Miss Marsh, and I am to escort you to the Empress immediately,' he said.

Valerie was very surprised. She had thought that she would be met by Anna Vyrubova. She was even more surprised when the officer turned and strode away, forcing her to scurry after his retreating back. Were all Russian gentlemen so impolite?

But in that short introduction she had noticed that his hair was a very dark brown beneath his flat-topped hat, his eyes were a vivid blue in his lean sun-tanned face, and he spoke very good English.

Pyotr Silakov's white cavalry jacket was decorated with gold epaulettes on his broad shoulders, and gold buttons on his chest, and his deep blue breeches were thrust into long black riding boots that sported silver spurs.

Being the only child of a hard-working vicar in south London, Valerie tried not to be overawed by her magnificent companion. But when she saw the shiny black motor car standing in the yard with a chauffeur at the wheel, she could not contain her excitement.

'I have never sat in a motor car before!' she exclaimed, as the man-servant opened the door and she climbed into the gleaming leather interior.

'Have you not?' Pyotr Silakov seemed bored by her delight and took his seat beside her without further comment.

'Tell me about Tsarskoe Selo, please.' Valerie was determined to enjoy her drive to the Imperial palace, and hoped that her companion's cool behaviour would warm a little when she showed genuine interest in her new surroundings.

Looking down at the small, dowdily dressed female beside him, Pyotr heaved a sigh of silent distaste. Miss Marsh was not only a foreigner, but an English one, at that, and now she wanted to talk, which only added to his annoyance.

Pyotr had learned English at school and was good at the language, but once his regiment moved out to Tsarskoe Selo and he found favour with the Tsar, he heard the alien tongue spoken far too often for his liking.

Due to Empress Alexandra, who was a granddaughter of Queen Victoria, everything English was admired these days. There were English chintzes in the Imperial apartments, English furniture in all the rooms and, more irritating than anything else, English was spoken continually between the Tsar and his wife.

Thank heavens the grand duchesses and their brother spoke together in their native tongue, but Pyotr was not at all happy about this intrusion by an English girl.

Miss Marsh had no title, she was obviously without means judging by the appalling way in which she dressed, and she was now to be planted in the midst of the young Romanovs to encourage them to speak *more* English.

'Tsarskoe Selo translates as 'the Tsar's village',' said Pyotr crisply, 'and there are two Imperial palaces at the centre of the park. One is the huge Catherine Palace and the smaller one is Alexander Palace, where we are going now.'

'And where I will meet Grand Duchess Olga,' said Valerie, with a smile. 'Do you have much contact with the Imperial family?' She did not know what to call him. Mister didn't sound right. Should she call him sir? She turned her head to look up at him. 'I hear they are a most devoted family. There are four daughters, are there not? And the one boy is the youngest?'

Pyotr nodded. 'Alexis Nicolaievich is Sovereign Heir Tsarevich, Grand Duke of Russia, and nine years old.'

Valerie pondered. 'What is the simplest name I can call him?' she asked. These Russian names seemed incredibly long to her.

'You may speak of him as the tsarevich, but must always address him as Your Imperial Highness, if he speaks to you.'

She inclined her head. 'Grand Duchess Olga is eighteen, the same age as me. How old are the other girls?'

'Tatiana is sixteen, Marie is fourteen, and Anastasia is twelve,' he said. 'Now look out of the window, Miss Marsh, we are entering the Imperial park.'

Obediently Valerie gazed out at the high iron fence that surrounded the park. Two Cossack horsemen in scarlet tunics, black fur caps and boots, with shining sabres at their sides, were riding around the outside of the fence.

'Are they on guard?' she asked.

'The Cossacks are on continual patrol around the park,' said Pyotr. 'And within the grounds are hundreds of infantrymen, who make up the Imperial Guard, as well as some

4

cavalry detachments. One of which is mine.'

Looking again at the animated face beside him, he noticed for the first time the luminosity of her grey eyes and the softness of her upturned mouth. She was not beautiful, but very feminine despite her dreary grey-blue coat and schoolgirl's hat. Fleetingly he wondered what colour hair she possessed for not a strand was visible beneath the thick felt on her head.

Pyotr Silakov began to appear almost human now. 'Where is your home?' she asked. 'Have you any brothers or sisters?'

Valerie liked people, and had often helped her father with the poor and needy in his parish of Putney. She enjoyed talking to them and hearing about their lives.

'My home is in the Ukraine,' said Pyotr, his voice showing affection for the first time, 'on our estate near Kamenka. It is called Mavara.'

'Mavara? What a lovely name.'

Miss Marsh might be a foreigner, but she appeared to be reasonably intelligent.

'And I have one sister,' he went on, 'called Tassya. She was hurt in a riding accident three years ago and is paralysed from the waist down.'

'Oh no!' Valerie bit at her bottom lip. 'Can nothing be done to heal her?'

Pyotr shook his head. 'A little wooden chair

has been made for her and her maid-servant pushes her wherever she wishes to go.'

'Poor Tassya. I cannot imagine how dreadful it must be not to walk.'

'Or ride,' he said. 'She was a wonderful horsewoman in the old days and would often beat me when we raced together.'

But that was Life, thought Pyotr. Tragedies had to be accepted. It was the Will of God. Even the Imperial family with all their fame and fortune were not free from grief.

'Here we are, Miss Marsh.'

Thankfully they had arrived at their destination, and as the man-servant went round to open Valerie's door, Pyotr climbed out on the other side.

In a few short minutes the little stranger had discovered far too much about him, and had even made him forget his dislike of her. If they had travelled together for very much longer *he* might have shown interest in *her*, and that would have been insane.

Count Pyotr Silakov had to marry a wealthy woman. A great deal of money was needed for his crumbling estate, and to care for his crippled sister in the future.

As Valerie stood gazing up at the palace with its brickwork of yellow and white designed in simple classical style, Pyotr collected his thoughts.

'We are going to the right wing, Miss Marsh,' he said, 'which houses the private apartments of the Imperial family.'

With her heart beating a little faster, Valerie followed him through a polished hallway and along a richly carpeted corridor. There were footmen everywhere, standing before closed doors, and opening others as she and the cavalry officer advanced. But not a word was spoken and some were standing at such rigid attention they could have been mistaken for statues.

Then another door was flung open and she was there.

Valerie entered a big room that was filled with comfortable armchairs and several sofas. Low, white-draped tables were set in front of various chairs, and on them were glasses in long silver holders and plates of biscuits.

When a tall figure moved forward from the far end of the room, Valerie found herself curtseying to Empress Alexandra as Pyotr Silakov bowed beside her.

'Valerie Marsh,' said a quiet voice, 'I hope you are not too weary from your travels. Please be seated. We will have tea when my family join us and then Olga will take you upstairs. Thank you, Count Silakov,' she inclined her head at the young officer, 'you may now return to your duties.'

He was a count! Thank heavens she hadn't called him Mister, thought Valerie. Then she turned her attention to the Empress of all the Russias and her companion, Anna Vyrubova.

The Empress was wearing a loose, flowing white robe trimmed at her throat and waist with lace. And as she spoke to Anna, Valerie admired her thick shiny hair, which was coiled into a bun at the back of her neck.

Far tidier than mine, she decided, and wished she could have a wash and brush-up. But her coat and hat had been taken by one of the footmen, and the Empress had not given permission for her to leave the room. She wouldn't have known where to go, anyway.

Gritting her teeth and hoping it would not be long to tea-time as she was feeling extremely hungry, Valerie went on studying her companions.

Empress Alexandra was very tall and straight-backed, wearing white pointed shoes with low heels. She had a pleasant voice and moved gracefully, seating herself on the sofa between Valerie's chair and Anna's. But she did not smile and Valerie was surprised by her sad expression.

Anna Vyrubova was very different and Valerie would have liked to speak to her. It was Anna's original idea that had started this exciting adventure from England. But the Empress claimed Anna's full attention so Valerie could only look at the large soft lady dressed in navy blue, and listen as she answered the Empress in her breathless, little girl's voice.

When Grand Duchess Olga came in, it was quite a relief. Valerie felt instantly relaxed in the company of a young and amiable person.

'I am so glad to meet you, Valerie,' said Olga, coming to sit beside her on another upright chair. 'And I want you to tell me all about your life in Putney.' She had thick chestnut-brown hair and blue eyes, and a warm smile, which lit up her broad Russian face. 'I expect all this will seem very strange to you at first, but you'll soon get used to our large family and feel at home here.'

'I'm sure I will be happy here,' said Valerie, smiling back, 'and I hope to learn Russian very quickly. Your knowledge of *my* language puts me to shame!'

Olga laughed and then introduced her to the rest of the family as they came in.

Tatiana was tall and elegant like her mother. Marie had the largest blue eyes that Valerie had ever seen. And Anastasia was short and cheerful and brown-haired.

When Tsar Nicholas came to join them, Valerie rose and curtsied again. His smile was as warm as Olga's, and his English was perfect.

It soon became clear that he and the Empress were devoted to each other and the whole family adored the handsome, auburn-haired tsarevich, Alexis, who came in last of all.

Valerie wasn't sure if such adoration was good for the blue-eyed boy, who seemed a little wild and wilful to her; after her upbringing of self-restraint in the quiet vicarage, such behaviour seemed indulgent.

But perhaps such affection was to be expected towards the heir to the throne, and they were certainly a very happy family.

During the surprisingly modest repast, with tea being poured into the long glasses, no milk, and biscuits being the only form of nourishment, Valerie remembered Mrs Duffy's fruit cakes and scones with longing.

Although there was only money for necessities at home, Mrs Duffy, who had been their housekeeper for as long as Valerie could remember, always made sure that their stomachs were full.

Here, at Alexander Palace, she accepted two glasses of hot tea and nibbled on a biscuit, hoping it wouldn't be too long before supper.

When the Tsar left the room, the young

people also stood up and departed for their own rooms on the floor above.

'Now that we are older Tatiana and I have our own bedrooms,' Olga said, leading Valerie along a wide corridor. 'But until recently we shared a room, as the two youngest do now.'

'And the tsarevich has his own room up here?'

'Of course!' Olga stared at Valerie. 'Alexis will be the next tsar of Russia and has a complete suite of rooms at the end of this passage. Our brother must be treated with special consideration as well as — ' she paused, then changed the subject. 'Now, here is my room, Valerie.'

She led the way into a charming bedroom, with icons and paintings on the walls, and a magnificent white bearskin rug on the bare floorboards.

'Your room is next door,' said Olga, 'and please tell me if there is anything you want. My maid will look after us both.'

Valerie was delighted with her room. Although simply furnished it was far more comfortable and feminine than her cold, stark room at home. The bed was covered with a white quilt embroidered with vine leaves. The dressing-table was frilled with the same green and white. And on the floor she, too, had a bearskin close to the bed.

How good it would feel on a cold winter's morning to put her feet on that fur and curl her toes into its softness. The food here might not be as good as Mrs Duffy's, but her bedroom was pure luxury.

★ ★ ★

Next morning Valerie and Olga sat sewing together in the girls' private sitting-room. Tatiana and the others were still at their lessons but Olga, being the eldest, didn't have to study so much and could spend time practising her English with Valerie.

She wanted to know about Valerie's connection with Mrs Lees, the banker's wife, who had accompanied her from England as far as St Petersburg.

'My mother and Mrs Lees were childhood friends,' said Valerie. 'And when my mother died, Mrs Lees wanted me to visit her, but I wouldn't leave Father at such a time.'

However, nine months later came a letter from Anna Vyrubova. Anna had long had dealings with Mr Lees at the bank and she was, moreover, the Empress's best friend.

Anna explained that the young duchesses led very secluded lives out at Tsarskoe Selo, and she had suggested to the Empress that the friendship of an English girl, of good family and education, would be an excellent idea for a year, or so. The Empress had agreed.

'My father persuaded me that such an opportunity should not be missed,' Valerie said. 'And he has Mrs Duffy to take care of him, so I said yes.'

'I am so glad that Mrs Duffy is there and you are here with us,' said Olga.

The grand duchess was so pretty and warm-hearted, Valerie wondered if she had any male friends.

'Do you meet many young noblemen?' she asked, hoping Olga would not be offended by the question.

Olga looked across at Valerie with intense blue eyes.

'There has been some talk of Crown Prince Carol of Romania,' she said. 'But Papa thinks I am too young to worry about such matters and I won't leave Russia, Valerie.' It was the first time she had spoken so passionately. 'I have told Papa I am a Russian and will *remain* a Russian.'

'What about the handsome soldiers I see guarding the palace? They are all Russian, aren't they? Though I suppose even high-ranking officers are not the right quality for a grand duchess?'

She was thinking of Count Pyotr Silakov.

Olga shook her head. 'They would not be suitable for any of us,' she said. 'But what about you, Valerie? Is there a gentleman waiting for you back in England? Or would you like to be introduced to some of our splendid Russian men?'

Valerie blushed. 'I don't know anyone special at home,' she said, 'but a very handsome officer met me at the railway station and escorted me here. His name was Count Pyotr Silakov.'

'Excellent!' cried Olga, putting down her sewing and clapping her hands. 'A titled gentleman to escort you to the Grand Ball at the Winter Palace.'

'What is the Grand Ball?' Valerie was surprised by Olga's enthusiasm. 'And I don't have the right clothes for a very special occasion. Besides, the count may be married. He wasn't very friendly when we got talking in the motor car.'

'I shall ask Papa to find out if this count has a wife. Then, if not, Papa must command him to partner you at the Ball. The Grand Ball is held in the Winter Palace in St Petersburg,' she explained, 'and marks the beginning of the season. And do not worry about clothes, dear Valerie. If you cannot borrow something suitable from me, one of our seamstresses will make you a beautiful gown.'

Valerie closed her eyes. To be invited to the Grand Ball in St Petersburg was exciting enough. But to go on the arm of a young and handsome count would be the most romantic thing that had ever happened to her. Just wait till her father and Mrs Duffy heard about that!

She opened her eyes and looked across at Olga.

'I still cannot believe I am here,' she said.

'You are really and truly here,' said Olga, with a contented little nod, 'and your new life has only just begun, Valerie Marsh. You have still to meet our beloved holy man.'

'Holy man?' said Valerie. 'Do you mean a priest? Or a monk?'

'Just a very ordinary man,' said Olga, 'a peasant, really. But one with God-given powers. Now, no more surprises or your poor head will burst!' She stood up and moved across to take Valerie's hand. 'Come on, English girl, let's go out for a walk in the fresh air and see if you can point out your handsome count to me!'

2

'You are not yourself this evening, Petya,' remarked Andrei Odarka, who was also a cavalry officer in the Tsar's service. Both men were bachelors and shared a spacious apartment overlooking the Imperial park. 'Can it be the arrival of the English girl that has disturbed you?'

'Have you seen her?' Pyotr turned his bright eyes on Andrei and looked at him properly for the first time that evening.

Andrei was relieved to see his friend appearing more normal. The last hour had been passed without a word being spoken and Andrei had begun to wonder if his companion were in a trance.

'I have seen a small insignificant person with Grand Duchess Olga,' said Andrei. 'There is nothing striking about Miss Marsh, Petya.'

'She is not beautiful — hardly pretty,' admitted Pyotr, 'yet I cannot get her out of my mind.'

Since that first meeting he had seen Valerie Marsh at a distance on several occasions, walking with the grand duchess, and to his

16

astonishment Pyotr had wanted to know her better.

'Certainly not beautiful,' agreed Andrei, with a grin, 'and owner of the most dreary apparel. Why should such an uninteresting female attract your attention, Petya?'

Pyotr frowned. What was it about the English girl that so disconcerted him? She was very small with an upright carriage and light, dainty footsteps. But most of all it was the calm of her grey eyes and the sweetness of her lips that fascinated him. He was not accustomed to such serenity in a female face.

His mother, Countess Irina, was a hard embittered woman, immensely strong both mentally and physically, who ran the family estate in the Ukraine as forcefully as any man. She had learnt to live that way ever since her husband had gambled away the Silakov fortune and then shot himself, unable to face the mountain of debts.

Grimly his widow had carried on alone, determined that her son should wed an heiress in due time. Money was desperately needed at Mavara and could only be obtained by the dowry of a rich bride.

Pyotr sighed, stretching out his long legs in the armchair and wishing life were not so complicated. Why should he have to marry a woman because of her wealth? And why were his thoughts continually returning to the dowdily dressed English girl, whose interest in everything around her had been so warm and delightful?

'You are not listening, Petya,' said his friend again.

'I am sorry, Andrei.' Pyotr turned his head to smile at the patient, fair-haired man who was sitting in the armchair beside him. 'I promise to give you my closest attention from now on. What is it you wish to say?'

'I was saying that I hoped you would forget all about this foreigner and not catch sight of her again,' said Andrei. 'We are both attending the Grand Ball at the Winter Palace, and you will not be seeking a suitable heiress if your mind is forever returning to Miss Marsh.'

★　★　★

At the beginning of November snow began to fall, and overnight Tsarskoe Selo turned into a sparkling white fairyland. The motor cars vanished, and horse-driven sleighs and toboggans took their place. Morning lessons were curtailed, and the whole family went outside into the clear crisp air.

When the skies became overcast, or blizzards raged, life in Alexander Palace returned to normal, but on sunny days Valerie saw everyone put on his or her boots and furs and go outside.

One morning she was watching as the grand duchesses fitted skis to their boots, and the Empress was helped into a small horse-driven sleigh to take a drive around the park.

The Tsar was also there and, to Valerie's surprise, was busily shovelling snow away from the paths. The tsarevich was with him and Tsar Nicholas was showing his son the best way to lift and hold the long-handled shovel.

Servants and guards were all around, enjoying the snow as much as the Imperial family. Valerie stood — warmly clad in her grey wool coat and mittens, but with a beaverskin hat from Olga on her head — absorbing the lively scene.

'How do you like our Russian winter, Miss Marsh?' asked a voice behind her, and she spun round having been unaware that anyone had joined her.

'You made me jump!' she said, thankful that the sudden rush of blood to her cheeks could be explained by fright, for the handsome officer was standing very close behind her, in a long dark green overcoat and black fur hat. 'I love every minute of my new life, thank you, Count Silakov.'

Pyotr smiled for the first time, his teeth very white in his suntanned face.

'For how long will you be staying in my country, Miss Marsh?'

'For one year,' she said, 'unless the Imperial family wish me to remain for longer.'

Pyotr decided that the beaverskin hat suited her much better than the grey felt she had worn last time he saw her.

'Valerie — look at this!' Olga's voice interrupted them. 'It is not difficult and you should have a go.'

The grand duchess arrived with a flurry of snow as she drew her skis together and halted in front of them, panting and laughing.

Pyotr bowed.

'You are Count Pyotr Silakov?' said Olga, glancing up at the tall young officer and realizing why Valerie found him attractive.

'That is my name. Always at your service, Your Imperial Highness,' he said, bowing again.

'For goodness sake call me Olga Nicolaievna in simple Russian fashion,' said Olga. 'It is only on grand occasions that my full title is used, and even then it embarrasses me, Count Silakov.'

'Why Nicolaievna?' asked Valerie, wondering how she would ever learn all about the

Russians and their language, yet eager to gather all the information she could about this fascinating land.

'Because it is my patronym — my father's name — like yours is Marsh,' said the grand duchess. 'Now, Valerie dear, I will leave you with the count, if he can spare the time?'

Pyotr smiled down at her.

'I am off duty for the next two hours, Olga Nicolaievna,' he said, 'and will gladly walk with Miss Marsh.'

They both turned to look at Valerie, whose face had become pink again at this suggestion.

'If the grand duchess wishes to go on skiing, I shall be delighted to walk at a slower pace,' she said.

★　★　★

That morning spent with Count Pyotr Silakov walking in the Imperial park, was one of the happiest times Valerie could remember. Now that his initial coldness had disappeared, she really enjoyed the company of the young count.

And Pyotr was both stimulated and entertained by her.

He wanted to know all about life in

21

England and how it compared to the Russian way of living. He asked what things she found better here and what she did not like at all. He even laughed out loud when Valerie confessed to disliking the cabbage soup and boiled fish that appeared all too often at mealtimes, and said how she missed Mrs Duffy's roast beef on Sunday.

'It is hard on the Palace chef,' said Pyotr, 'for it is said that the Tsar is fondest of the peasant's simple cooking, and the Empress is not interested in food at all.'

'Do not think me too critical of your land,' said Valerie quickly. 'There is much to enjoy here.'

'I asked for your opinion and am glad you felt able to speak so freely,' Pyotr said.

'There is one thing that puzzles me,' Valerie went on.

'And what is that, Miss Marsh?'

'Why does the Empress look so sad?'

Pyotr sighed as their boots crunched along the path in unison.

'No doubt Olga Nicolaievna will tell you in time,' he said. 'But as it is now common knowledge in Court circles I might as well inform you, myself.'

He explained that the tsarevich suffered from haemophilia. Any fall, or cut, which started bleeding could be fatal to the boy.

'He is watched all the time and understands his own problems but still manages to injure himself sometimes,' said Pyotr.

'How terrible!' Valerie thought of all the pain and anxiety for both Alexis and his loving family, when such an accident occurred.

'The tsarevich's plight has been kept secret for years because it is not the condition one would choose for the future Tsar of all the Russias,' said Pyotr grimly. 'But the boy has been ill so often of late that we all know of it here. That is the reason for his mother's sorrow, Miss Marsh.'

'Is there no cure?'

Pyotr shrugged. 'The Empress is very religious and sets much store on prayer and faith-healing. And some say the peasant Grigorii Rasputin, helps the boy at times. But I do not believe it. Now,' he went on briskly, 'enough has been said on that subject and we are almost back at the palace. Do not say that I have told you about the tsarevich, please, Miss Marsh. Let the news come to you from Olga Nicolaievna when she feels ready to speak.'

'I won't say a word, but thank you for telling me.'

Warmed by the English girl's sincerity and compassion, Pyotr watched as she disappeared across the forecourt, straight-backed and light-footed, despite her heavy winter boots. And he realised he was becoming perilously fond of the little foreigner.

Later that month, an invitation arrived for Valerie from Anna Vyrubova, asking her to come and take tea in her house which was close to the palace.

Valerie had seen Anna several times during the past weeks, but as she was always in the company of the Empress they had not spoken to each other. Now, an afternoon spent with the lady in her own home, would be a splendid opportunity to know her better.

Warmly wrapped against the bitter cold, Valerie set off for Anna's house which was but a few minutes walk away. Halfway between the two buildings she almost bumped into Pyotr, who was also on foot striding towards her through the snow.

'Miss Marsh! What are you doing out here in this cold wind?' He halted in front of her. 'Another blizzard is expected and you should not be out alone in this weather. You might lose your way.'

'I would be very stupid to lose my way even in a snowstorm,' said Valerie, smiling at the look of concern on his face. 'I am going to Anna Vyrubova's for tea and it is that house there, isn't it?'

Pyotr nodded, still looking perturbed. 'You

are visiting Anna Vyrubova?' he repeated, his dark brows drawn together in a frown. 'Has she invited you?'

'Of course.' The brusqueness of his tone had surprised her. 'I wouldn't go without an invitation.'

'I wish you were not going,' he said. 'That lady has some strange friends.'

'But Grand Duchess Olga knows about it and wished me a happy time.' Valerie stared at the man. 'Goodness, Count Silakov, you do say some extraordinary things. Anna is so well known at the palace I'm certain her friends would be acceptable to the Empress.'

'It is one particular friend who troubles me. Has the grand duchess mentioned the name Rasputin to you?'

Valerie shook her head.

'Then beware of Grigorii Rasputin, Miss Marsh.' Pyotr's eyes were as cold and bleak as the snow-laden sky as he looked down at her. 'I am sure he will be at this tea party, and I am also sure that he is dangerous. I beg you to have a care and shield yourself against this peasant.'

Rasputin was known and disliked by all. But as long as he found favour with the Empress and her family, his visits had to be tolerated.

Suddenly Valerie remembered Olga telling

her about a holy man. An ordinary man, Olga had said, but one with God-given powers. Was Grigorii Rasputin this man?

Shrugging her shoulders in bewilderment, Valerie assured Pyotr that she would take care, then left him to walk up the path to Anna's little house.

Thank heavens the count had not been invited to the tea party, she thought. He would have ruined her enjoyment of the afternoon and any meeting she might have with the intriguing peasant.

★　★　★

Valerie would never forget the first time she met the holy man, Grigorii Rasputin. His powerful presence was so fascinating that she took in little of her surroundings. Anna's house was painted white on the outside and only one storey high, but the parlour in which they gathered was almost bursting with the personality of the man.

Anna spoke in whispers, her eyes never leaving the visitor who sat solid, and deeply relaxed, in a chair by the fire.

'I shall translate for you,' she said to Valerie.

Rasputin wore a long black robe with black breeches above black leather boots. A brown belt held the robe in place for there did not appear to be any buttons or fastenings, and on his broad chest glinted a heavy gold cross.

'This is Valerie Marsh from England,' said Anna, as the girl's hand was taken in a large warm grasp and she felt light-coloured eyes pierce into her very soul.

In that first moment of greeting Valerie felt as if Grigorii Rasputin knew her thoughts, her history, everything about her. Yet she was not afraid. She was comforted and reassured, and a glow of affection began to burn within her as she smiled at the seated man.

Dangerous? The count must have been thinking of someone else. Or was he jealous of the holy man's contact with the Imperial family? Certainly Olga had spoken of the man with great fondness. And there was something godly about his penetrating eyes and enthralling presence.

Rasputin spoke in a thick Siberian accent, but Anna relayed to Valerie that he was pleased to meet someone from such a far away country, that he could tell she was a good girl born of good parents, and she would find happiness with the man she loved after many difficulties had been overcome.

How did he know so much? Valerie fell on her knees beside his chair, wanting to stay close to him as a wonderful peace spread through her body.

Her mother had been, and her father most certainly was, a really good person. And *she* always tried to be kind and considerate towards others. But Valerie was not sure about the man she was supposed to love. She found Count Pyotr Silakov very attractive, but she couldn't say she loved him.

'I am a disciple,' whispered Anna beside her. 'And I believe you have become one of us, dear.'

Valerie nodded. 'I have never felt so content,' she said wanting to reach out and touch the man again.

Grigorii Rasputin was not handsome. His long brown hair was parted in the middle and straggled onto his shoulders. And his skin was an unhealthy yellow above his beard, as if he did not go out-of-doors much.

But his light eyes were hypnotic and Valerie was filled with a tranquillity she had never experienced before.

'Tell him I am also a disciple, Anna Vyrubova.'

'I knew our Father Grigorii would affect you!' cried Anna. 'He is easy to find if you wish to see him again, dear,' she went on, after listening to the holy man's reply. 'He has an apartment in St Petersburg where we are always welcome.'

'Where does he come from, Anna? He doesn't speak the Russian I am used to hearing at the palace.'

'His home is in a small village beyond the Ural mountains,' said Anna.

At that moment a servant entered the room bringing in the tea. Then she moved across to light the lamps on the wide shelf by the window.

'Father Grigorii travels home every spring and summer,' Anna went on, as she poured tea from the samovar then carried a glass in its silver holder across to the holy man. She returned to join Valerie at the table and poured her out a glass. 'He gathers strength there before returning to the capital,' she said.

'I should like to see his home.' It would be like a pilgrimage. 'Could we go there together, Anna?'

The older woman frowned. 'You must ask the Empress, Valerie. But as you came to Russia for Olga Nicolaievna, I think she will want you to travel with the family down to the Crimea for Easter, then to Poland in the summer.'

'Oh, there is so much to see and do here I shall *never* manage all the things I long to experience before going home!' cried Valerie.

Rasputin stirred at the sound of her voice

and Anna turned her head to listen.

'He says do not distress yourself, little one. You will achieve all you desire in due time.' She paused, as the man's thick jerking words went on. 'He says you are a very loving, very restful person, and the man you love is blessed indeed.' Anna turned back to Valerie with curious eyes. 'Who is this man, dear? Have you a beau in England who is missing you?'

Valerie shook her head. That part of the holy man's knowledge was not correct. But maybe he was speaking about the future? How good it would be to think of someone loving her as much as she loved him; to have a union as steadfast as her parents' marriage had been.

'I do not know who Father Grigorii means,' she said gently, as she stood up. 'But I must return to the palace now. Please tell him that I am honoured to have made his acquaintance.'

She moved forward to catch hold of the holy man's hand and raised it to her lips. Then she thanked Anna Vyrubova for inviting her and made her careful way back in the snow, her mind filled with happy thoughts.

Olga wanted to hear all about Valerie's meeting with Grigorii Rasputin, and did not seem at all surprised by her news.

'He is a man of God and a miracle worker,' she said. 'Father Grigorii knows everything. Now I have more exciting news for you. I had words with Papa this afternoon and he has agreed to Count Silakov escorting you to the Grand Ball at the Winter Palace. The count is not married so it is quite in order for him to partner you. If Mrs Lees is in agreement. Perhaps *he* is your future husband, Valerie?'

Valerie blushed as she shook her head. But deep down she wondered, remembering the holy man's surprising wisdom.

★   ★   ★

'Petya, you are mad!' said Andrei Odarka. 'How can you escort the English girl to the Grand Ball!'

Andrei was worried about his friend and anxiety showed in his clear grey eyes.

'It is by order of the Tsar,' said Pyotr, in mock surprise. 'How can I refuse a Royal Command?'

'I believe you are becoming attracted to this female, Petya, and that is a most alarming position to be in.'

'I am not losing my heart to Miss Marsh,' said Pyotr. 'Although I admit to finding her an interesting little person. I want only to share her delight in my beloved Russia for a while. Can you not understand that?'

He studied his companion's troubled face.

'Are you not proud of Russia, Andrei? Would you not want the outside world to know us better? I want this girl to go back to England filled with memories of her time here, and I want her to tell everyone that Russia is a magnificent land.'

Andrei shrugged. 'There speaks the true patriot,' he said.

'I want Miss Marsh to experience all the glamour and gaiety of St Petersburg, and then I intend inviting her to Mavara,' said Pyotr. 'It will give Tassya much joy to see a new face and to practise her English. She is lonely out there on the estate. And a visit to the Ukraine will give Miss Marsh a chance to see a different part of this great continent.'

'You would take the English girl to meet your mother?' Andrei was shocked. Pyotr was really behaving most oddly.

Pyotr nodded. 'I intend enjoying a few more months of freedom before I have to marry an heiress and then *everyone* will be happy.'

3

St Petersburg

The following month Valerie travelled to the capital to stay with Mr and Mrs Lees, the English couple who had arranged her journey from England.

The first momentous event was to be the Grand Ball at the Winter Palace, escorted by Count Pyotr Silakov. After that, she was to remain with the Lees for a few more days and be shown around St Petersburg.

Olga Nicolaievna had been as excited as Valerie about her forthcoming adventure.

'You will love St Petersburg,' she said. 'How I *wish* that I were a mere nobody and could explore the shops and the markets like you, Valerie. See as much as you can and then come back and tell me all about it.'

'I will,' promised Valerie.

'First we must make sure you are suitably attired for the Ball,' went on the grand duchess. 'All the ladies will be wearing their finest gowns and you must be no exception.'

As Valerie journeyed to St Petersburg, she thought of the dress that Olga had insisted on her wearing. It was of white satin that clung tightly to her slender form. All the unmarried girls wore white, Olga informed her. It was cut very low and Valerie was glad that neither her father, nor Mrs Duffy, would see her so attired for the dress showed her bare shoulders, and more than enough of her small pointed breasts.

But Olga had declared that it was quite correct, with a long train sweeping behind her, and Olga must know.

The grand duchess also lent her some jewellery, making Valerie feel as if she came from the nobility herself, and she hoped Count Pyotr Silakov would be impressed.

She had also been given a maid of her own, called Dashka.

'Mama says Dashka must accompany you when you travel and make sure you are properly attended to at the Lees' establishment,' said Olga.

Valerie was very amused.

She had never possessed a maid servant before and had frequently run errands for her father on her own, all over town. But here in Russia she was learning to adapt to new rules and new ways of living, and was not missing her old life one little bit.

When she arrived at the Lees' fine white house on Vassily Island, north of the river

Neva, Valerie was enthralled by the view from her bedroom window, which looked out onto the frozen waters of Nicholas Quay.

Mr Lees told her that the next time she came to stay it should be in the spring, for then the ice would have melted and activity returned to the river with the arrival of foreign ships and their cargoes.

The Englishman had fallen in love with St Petersburg and enjoyed having an interested guest to impress with his knowledge of the city. He told her that it had been founded in 1703 by Peter the Great, and was made up of nineteen islands, all of which had been claimed back from swamp-land. Thousands of labourers had been employed to drain the swamps and to transport building materials, and eventually St Petersburg had risen above the water to stand in magnificent splendour.

A young Italian, named Rastrelli, had done most of the architecture, Mr Lees explained, and it was his fantastic style that now decorated the many spires and towers and onion domes with their colours of yellow, and sky blue, and Venetian red.

'And, of course, the green of the Winter Palace,' he said, 'where you will be going tomorrow night.'

*   *   *

The following evening Mrs Lees and Dashka spent over two hours helping Valerie to dress.

'I wish your dear mother were alive to see you here today,' said the banker's wife, her pale eyes awash with tears. 'And to know that you are a friend of Grand Duchess Olga, and have been invited to the Grand Ball, which opens the season in St Petersburg. How very proud she would be.'

'I shall write to Father and tell him all my news,' said Valerie. Although she didn't think her elderly, over-worked father would understand what she was trying to explain.

Russia was a dramatic land filled with vibrant colours, snow, furs, and biting cold. It was quite impossible for a weary vicar in grey old Putney to comprehend unless he was the possessor of a vivid imagination, and imagination was something Reverend Marsh had always lacked.

'You look like a princess,' declared Mrs Lees, dabbing at her eyes with a lace handkerchief. 'Now do take care, Valerie, and don't trip over that train going up and down stairs, will you, dear?'

Valerie smiled. 'Don't worry, Mrs Lees, Grand Duchess Olga taught me how to hold the train properly when I sit down, and when I dance, and I shall be very well escorted, besides.'

Dashka was not accompanying Valerie to the Ball and Mrs Lees felt happy with the arrangement made by the Tsar. If Tsar Nicholas considered it correct for Count Silakov to escort Valerie that evening, then who was she, a mere commoner, to query the Imperial decision?

Let *him* be proud of me, Valerie prayed, as a man servant knocked and announced that Count Silakov awaited them below.

Pyotr looked more handsome than ever when she went down to greet him in the hall, wearing full-dress uniform of scarlet jacket and immaculate elk-skin breeches. And she saw at once what a good impression the young officer was making on the English couple.

Valerie was also making an impact on the count in her ravishing white satin gown, and he wondered what Andrei Odarka's reaction would be on seeing her so attired. Gone was the dowdy Miss Marsh, and in her place was a stunning beauty with soft brown hair piled high on top of her small head, crowned with a diadem of pearls.

Little curls danced across her forehead, and her body looked deliciously slim and supple in its clinging satin. Valerie's waist was so narrow he could easily have encircled it with his hands, and around it she wore a rope of pearls caught on her hip with a buckle of diamonds.

Olga Nicolaievna had played a large part in this transformation, Pyotr decided, as he placed a long black velvet cloak around Valerie's shoulders.

After he had helped her into the waiting carriage and seated himself beside her, the coachman gave them extra furs to put over their knees for it was a freezing night. Then the man heaved himself up onto the high seat behind the horses, looking like an enormous shaggy bear, and they were off.

The Winter Palace, which took up three vast blocks along the waterfront, was suffused with light and Valerie saw that it was indeed all green and white as Mr Lees had told her. Baroque in style, it had an ornamental balustrade running along the front, topped by various white statues and urns.

In front of the palace, braziers were burning around the base of a tall, pink granite column erected in memory of Alexander 1, which was surmounted by the statue of a winged angel holding a cross.

Valerie's eyes danced with excitement as their carriage took its place in the line of many others, all waiting to present their occupants at the main entrance.

'I am glad there will be dancing,' Pyotr

said, looking down at his companion in the semi-darkness of the interior. 'I want to put my arms around your lovely body and hold it close to mine. I have never seen you before without layers of clothing and hats, Miss Marsh.'

'That is a most flirtatious remark, Count Silakov,' said Valerie, burying her chin into the folds of her velvet cloak and thankful he couldn't see the telltale reddening of her skin.

How very different he was now to the grim and rather disdainful cavalry officer, who had met her at Tsarskoe Selo railway station.

'It was meant to be flirtatious,' said Pyotr, slipping his hand beneath the furs and covering her fingers, in their long kid glove, with his own. 'Tonight you are for me, Miss Marsh, and we shall eat and drink and dance together without a care in the world.'

Looking up at him, feeling the warmth of his hand on hers, she smiled. 'Tonight is for us,' she agreed, and her heart began to thud beneath her bodice.

'Then you must call me Petya,' he said, 'because we are friends, and I will call you Varinka.'

'Varinka? I like that. It is softer, more musical than plain old Valerie.'

'Then come, Varinka, it is our time to alight.'

An attendant moved forward to open the carriage door for Valerie, then Pyotr followed her out and offered her his arm. Once inside the massive hallway another attendant came to take her cloak and for a moment she stood spellbound, gazing at the splendour around her.

Pyotr watched, amused by the rapture on her expressive face.

Great pillars of jasper, marble and malachite, supported the high gilded ceiling from which hung immense chandeliers of crystal and gold, and ahead of them rose a white marble staircase covered with a wine red carpet.

'Are you ready to ascend, Varinka?'

She nodded. 'It is not at all like Putney,' she said.

Up the grand staircase they floated, with Valerie's train slithering behind her and Pyotr's arm firm beneath her hand. Then she was jolted to a sudden standstill as an elderly general, his chest blazing with decorations, trod on her train causing her to exclaim and him to curse.

'I think you need to fold it over your arm, my dear Varinka,' said Pyotr.

Aware that she had forgotten Olga's careful advice, and dreadfully embarrassed at having caused such a fuss on the grand staircase,

Valerie looped the offending folds of material over her free arm, nodding and muttering apologies as she did so.

'Move on quickly,' she hissed at Pyotr, conscious of the critical gaze of other ladies who, glittering with diamonds, managed their own trains with delicate precision.

At the top of the staircase that branched to right and left, wide corridors stretched away with open doorways leading into state rooms, and others for dancing and dining. On the walls were baskets of orchids, and palm trees in large pots framed huge mirrors, but there was no time to stand and stare as Pyotr led her through the chattering throng towards one of the vast reception rooms.

It was there, in a chamber filled with guests, that Valerie was suddenly aware of being watched. Across from her, several paces away, stood a girl so tall that she could stare over the heads of most people. And she was looking at Valerie with the yellow eyes of a vigilant cat.

Heavens, thought Valerie, who is that?

For a moment she faltered. Her hand was still on Pyotr's arm but he had turned away from her and was talking to another officer on his left. The girl who was staring was also on the arm of a fair-haired officer, but although he was trying to gain her

41

attention she did not heed him.

'Miss Marsh, please will you meet my friend and fellow officer Igor Fateyev,' said Pyotr, introducing Valerie to his companion.

But the moment Igor Fateyev had bowed and taken his leave of them, Valerie turned her attention back to the tall female.

'Petya,' she said, 'who is that?'

The girl was wearing a gown of cream silk, the tone of which suited her black hair and almond skin to perfection. There were no diamonds around her neck but topazes as large as pigeons' eggs linked with a chain of gold. More yellow stones dangled from her ears and a gold band across her forehead bore one gleaming stone in the centre of her brow.

She possessed thick shiny black hair, which was coiled into a heavy knot at the back of her long neck, and she was the most striking female Valerie had ever seen. And the most unfriendly.

Pyotr had been unaware of Sophia's presence and as he caught sight of her he cursed Andrei for bringing her to this reception room. There were chambers enough for the guests to dine and dance in. Why had Andrei remained in this one so near the main staircase?

However, there was nothing Pyotr could do

about it so he led Valerie forward with a smile.

'Why, this is Sophia Lukaev, the beauty of St Petersburg,' he said easily. 'And this is another good friend of mine, Andrei Odarka. Perhaps you have already met Andrei out at Tsarskoe Selo, Miss Marsh?'

'I don't believe so.' Valerie inclined her head at the fair-haired man who was bowing smartly before her. Then she looked up into the yellow eyes of the raven-haired beauty.

'Sophia, this is Miss Valerie Marsh from England,' said Pyotr.

'Andrei told me.' Her unblinking stare took in every detail of the English girl's gown, and the pearls in her hair and around her waist.

The foreigner obviously had money, which was a danger in itself, but far worse was her air of innocence. This Valerie Marsh was the sort of female men would always find irresistible with her soft hair, and soft mouth, and cheeks as round and soft as peaches.

Sophia was angry. This newcomer was stealing the man she loved and flaunting herself on his arm so all could see and gossip about their friendship.

'I am pleased to make your acquaintance,' said Valerie, hoping they could now move on. She did not want the evening ruined by the animosity of this lovely girl.

43

Was Pyotr once her beau? Was Sophia still in love with him? Had Pyotr only agreed to escort *her* because the Tsar had ordered it?

Andrei also wanted to move away from Pyotr and his bewitching companion. What had happened to the dreary Miss Marsh? What bábka's spell had turned her into this shimmering vision of white satin and pearls?

'They are playing your favourite waltz, Sophia,' he said. 'Come and dance with me.'

Forcing a smile to her red lips, Sophia allowed herself to be led towards the nearest ballroom. But she was still fuming.

From the moment she was born Sophia Lukaev had been spoilt and adored by her parents, and she had grown up knowing she could have anything she wanted in life. When she was first introduced to Count Pyotr Silakov she had wanted him. She had wanted his title and she had wanted his love.

Patiently she had waited for his proposal of marriage, knowing that her parents, and the Countess Irina Silakov, approved of the match. Now Sophia stared with blank eyes straight ahead of her as Andrei ushered her forward. Somehow she must get Petya away from that little foreigner. He belonged to her.

Pyotr led Valerie in the opposite direction, out into a long corridor flowing with guests, and on to another ballroom.

'We will be dining with some other friends of mine, and their wives,' he said, as she remained silent. 'The saloon where we eat is over there so we can dance in this nearby chamber.'

He remained confident and at ease as they entered a huge crimson and gold ballroom where the chandeliers dripped with crystals. Looking up, Valerie thought they looked like icicles in the winter sunshine.

'Now, Varinka, smile and look happy,' he said, taking her hand as they joined a stream of dancers in the slow, processional steps of the polonaise.

'I would like to know about Sophia,' said Valerie. 'Is she a family friend? Have you known her long?'

'Ah, the Lukaev.' Pyotr shrugged. 'She is nothing, Varinka. Quite unimportant. The important one is *you*, my lovely one, and this evening of pleasure. We are here to enjoy ourselves, remember?'

Valerie pursed her lips. There was to be no explanation. Well, so be it. She would dance with Pyotr, and dine with him and his friends, and make the most of this historic occasion. Hopefully, she would not see that uncomfortable beauty again.

'Where are the Tsar and Empress Alexandra?' she asked, trying to concentrate on the haunting beat of the music. 'Olga said they would all be here tonight but I haven't seen them.'

'The Imperial family will be in the main reception room,' he said, 'meeting a long line of selected guests.'

'I am glad not to be royal,' said Valerie, 'and able to do most of the things I want to do.'

'Most?' said Pyotr. 'Why not *all* the things you want to do, Varinka?'

'Because there is so much to see and do before returning to England!'

'And what do you want most of all?' he asked.

They were waltzing now and Pyotr was holding her closer than was proper. She could feel the warmth of his body against her breasts and thighs and when she looked up his eyes caressed her lips, as if he wanted to kiss them.

Valerie swallowed hard and turned her head away, trying to gather her thoughts.

'I want to see more of Russia, and would dearly like to visit the birthplace of the holy man in Siberia.'

'Not that moujik again!' Pyotr loosened his hold on her and his blue eyes darkened with distaste. 'That peasant is no more holy than you or me, Varinka. I hope most sincerely you will remember my warning and have nothing more to do with him!'

'Of course he is holy! Anna Vyrubova and the Empress both think so and they cannot be wrong.'

'Nonsense. If you stay long enough in Russia, Valerie Marsh, you will learn exactly what kind of a man Rasputin really is.' Pyotr began to lead her away from the dance floor. 'Come, it is time to eat,' he said.

In the dining room she was introduced to two more officers and their wives, and they all sat at one of the many white-clothed tables and were served lobster salad and cold sturgeon and three kinds of caviar, followed by pastry tarts and whipped cream.

Valerie enjoyed the food, which was very different to the simple meals out at Tsarskoe Selo, but she couldn't follow the ebb and flow of conversation, so remained silent.

Once they had completed their repast, Pyotr bade his friends farewell and escorted Valerie back to the ballroom.

'Tonight,' he said, 'I will take you home in a sleigh. It will be extremely cold, but we will have plenty of furs to wrap around us, and I wish you to see the stars above St Petersburg. It will be a wonderful memory of this, our first night together, Varinka.'

They were dancing the mazurka and Valerie

was trying to remember the steps Olga had taught her.

'I don't know that there is much I *want* to remember,' she said. 'That meeting with the lady who obviously disliked me was a shock. And your prejudice against Father Grigorii was also upsetting. I thought I enjoyed your company, but this evening you have shown a less pleasing side to your nature.'

There. She had said it. And she didn't care if his pride had been hurt.

But Pyotr was surprisingly unabashed.

'Now, now, Varinka,' he said, 'you are making a mountain out of a bees' nest.'

'Out of a mole hill,' she snapped.

'A mole hill, yes.' He nodded. 'But once you know me better you will feel happier and not find insults in everything I say and do. Come.'

Although Valerie would have liked to dance some more, she was hustled out into the corridor and down the wide staircase with no time for further argument.

With the black cloak around her shoulders, Pyotr hurried her down the last steps, anxious to summon a sleigh. Other guests were also departing and, although a long line of carriages stood waiting, there were few sleighs about.

Fortunately he was able to attract the

attention of a brightly painted one, drawn by two black horses.

The driver was so heavily wrapped in his bearskin coat and cap that his face was almost invisible. But he clambered off and made sure Pyotr and Valerie were well covered in furs, with lambskins for their feet and extra pieces of fur tucked into the corner of the sleigh for warmth. Then he climbed back in front of them and flicked his reins over the horses' steaming backs.

They were off. The sleigh flew silently over the snow and quickly left the clear shovelled streets behind. Then the only sound was the cheerful jingling of the bells on the horses' harnesses, and the hissing of the metal runners as they slid over the frosted carpet beneath.

Cocooned in her mountain of furs, Valerie looked up at the starlit night and her annoyance died within her. To her right the river Neva shone like steel. Above her the moon illuminated the spires and gilded domes of many churches and made the roofs of palaces along the waterfront glisten and sparkle in turn.

'Is she not beautiful, my Russia?' whispered Pyotr beside her. 'Is this sleigh ride not something to remember, Varinka?'

She sighed and turned her head to look up

at him. This journey under the stars of St Petersburg *was* something very special, and she had to agree that *this* was worth remembering.

'Good.' Pyotr sounded very self-satisfied, but she was not going to let him irritate her again. 'Now, Varinka, I have been thinking of what you said and have decided to show you more of my beloved land. Soon I have some leave from duty, and wish to invite you to Mavara.'

She was snuggled beneath her furs like a small hibernating animal with only her eyes and little nose showing in the freezing air. But the sparkle had returned to her luminous eyes, which were almost black in the moonlight, and he caught a glimpse of her smile.

'Oh Petya, I would love to see Mavara! But is it right for me to have more days away from Tsarskoe Selo, when I should be spending time with Grand Duchess Olga?'

'I shall speak to the Empress,' he said, rejoicing in the fact that she was his enthusiastic and lovable Varinka once more. 'I will explain that as you are only in Russia for a short time, it is very important for you to see as much as possible of our great land.'

'If Empress Alexandra agrees, I shall be happy to visit your home, Petya.'

She was about to say more but he leaned over and cupped her face in his hands.

'Be silent,' he said, and covered her mouth with his.

She could feel the warmth of his body radiating through the folds of fur, then he was touching her closed mouth with the tip of his tongue, caressing, taunting, making her gasp. When his tongue entered her parted lips it flicked in and out, then around her little strong teeth until her tongue came to join his and she was weak with rapture.

Suddenly Valerie wanted to feel his hands on her body, wanted him to touch her breasts and stroke her trembling thighs. She ached to be rid of all the furs and restricting clothing and feeling Pyotr's skin against her own. She was hot and shaking and overwhelmed by a passion she had never known before.

Pyotr was laughing, amazed and delighted at the emotions he had aroused in her.

'Our time will come, my Varinka, do not fret.' He adjusted the furs around her before stroking back the curls on her brow and setting straight the diadem of pearls, which had fallen askew. 'But now we are approaching the house of your friends.'

Valerie blinked and put a hand to her head. Her bound locks were still in place, but her lips were burning and she prayed she did not

51

look too dishevelled.

The sleigh turned into Bolshoy Prospect and slid noiselessly up to the English couple's residence

'I will see you again, Varinka,' said Pyotr, scrambling out from beneath the furs and helping her onto the white, crystallized forecourt. 'I will see you again at Tsarskoe Selo.'

'Oh yes!' said Valerie, holding both his hands against her breast. 'I hope it will be soon, Petya!'

Then the footman opened the door to receive her into the warm hallway and Valerie left the man who had captured her heart.

Count Pyotr Silakov was the man Father Grigorii had meant. She was sure of that now.

As Dashka helped her to prepare for bed, Valerie thought of visiting Pyotr's home and meeting his mother and sister, and getting to know him better. She scarcely knew him as a person. But as a *man* she was totally devastated by him.

4

The following day, trying to put Pyotr to the back of her mind for a while, Valerie concentrated on the voluble Mrs Lees who was taking her shopping.

The Lees' coachman made sure the ladies were covered with several tartan rugs before he closed the door of the carriage, then went round to climb up onto his seat behind the horses.

Mrs Lees would not allow any furs within her conveyance.

'Nasty, uncivilised things and one can never be sure where they've been,' she told Valerie, pulling her tartan more closely round her maroon-clad body.

Mrs Lees' wide-brimmed velvet hat was also maroon with an ostrich-feather trim, and it made Valerie feel very inferior in her grey-blue woollen coat and grey felt hat.

But she had looked grand enough last night, she thought, hugging herself in silent pleasure as she remembered her satin gown, and the pearls, and the sleigh-ride back with Pyotr.

As Mrs Lees babbled on about how she

missed England, and how dreadfully cold it was during these long winter months, and how excruciatingly hot St Petersburg became in the summer, Valerie wished the lady would stop chattering.

She wanted to gaze out of the window and look at all the exciting things that were passing before her eyes. For this was Pyotr's beloved Russia and she wanted to see, and learn, everything possible for *his* sake now, as well as for her own.

'And the smells, dear,' went on the relentless voice beside her, 'during a heatwave are quite frightful with epidemics always raising their ugly heads. Usually it is cholera and we have to boil all our water — most tiresome,' said Mrs Lees, with a sniff. 'Of course, we go away for some of the time and I suppose you will be going with the Imperial family on one of their lengthy trips away from the heat and dust?'

Valerie nodded. 'Grand Duchess Olga mentioned a visit down to the Crimea at Easter, but I don't know about the summer.'

Perhaps Mavara? But she didn't mention Pyotr's invitation to Mrs Lees. She held the memory of last night close to her heart, still bemused by what had happened and the emotions he had aroused in her newly awakened body.

As they were crossing Nicholas Bridge with its splendid bronze griffons on the railings, Mrs Lees caught her attention once more.

'Have you seen much of Anna Vyrubova?' she asked. 'And has the name of that peculiar man from Siberia been mentioned?'

Valerie folded her hands neatly together on top of the rug and turned to look at her companion's inquisitive face. Mrs Lees had brought her to Russia, and was also providing her with a home during the few days she remained in the capital. The banker's wife was a kind, if irritating lady, and would naturally want to know all about life at Tsarskoe Selo.

'I have seen Anna Vyrubova several times,' said Valerie, 'and it was at her house that I was introduced to the holy man, Grigorii Rasputin.'

'You've met him!' Mrs Lees' voice rose to a shriek above the rattling of the carriage wheels. The snow had been swept off the streets down which they were travelling and piled between road and pavement, forming ramparts almost four feet high. 'Valerie, I beg you to be careful with that peasant. He has the most dreadful reputation: Dear me, I wish Mr Lees were here — he would know best how to manage this delicate matter.'

Valerie frowned. Why was everyone with

whom she now spoke so opposed to the holy man?

Mrs Lees' voice dropped to a whisper as she glanced at the front of the carriage, fearful lest the coachman should hear.

'I cannot speak of the immoral habits of that man. Holy, indeed! But I do assure you no lady is safe in his company and do not *ever* agree to visit him in his apartment, dear.'

Valerie stared. These were similar remarks to those made by Pyotr but she had thought he spoke from jealousy. Surely that was not a sin applicable to this decent English matron?

'The Empress is very fond of him and so is Anna,' she said. 'And you couldn't find two more respectable ladies, could you, Mrs Lees?'

Mrs Lees pursed her mouth. 'Empress Alexandra is not very highly thought of so far as *I* can gather, and they do keep themselves very hidden away out there at Tsarskoe Selo.' She changed the subject abruptly. 'And what about the young tsarevich? What do you think of him? There are many rumours about that boy, you know. Some say he is mad — others that he is deformed. Have you seen much of him, dear?'

Outside the carriage windows St Petersburg was standing in all its glory. The golden domes of cathedrals were shining in the wintry sunshine beside pillared porticos of romantic buildings, and many frozen waterways. Iron braziers were set up in side streets and glowed like red beacons in the snow, whilst in the parks men in great rough boots and sheepskins were making snow mountains for shouting children, who stood ready with their toboggans.

And Valerie had to sit and listen as her companion's voice rolled on as monotonously as the carriage wheels.

'I have seen Alexis only at meal times,' she said, 'as most of my time is spent with Grand Duchess Olga.'

'But what does he look like?' persisted Mrs Lees. 'Is he physically maimed? He will be the next tsar, you know.'

'I know that, and Alexis is a most handsome child — as are all the family. Ah, is this Nevsky Prospect?' Thank heavens they had arrived.

'I would rather have Regent Street any day,' said Mrs Lees. 'But Nevsky Prospect is supposed to be the longest and widest street in the world and stretches from Alexander Gardens, which we passed just now, all the way down to the Moscow Gate.'

There were many people about, all heavily clad in long fur coats and boots, some skimming along the side in sleighs, which made Valerie's heart leap at memories of the previous night and others looking less at ease in laboriously drawn carriages, like their own.

'The shops here are quite pleasant,' said Mrs Lees, 'and I am taking you to Alexandre's, which is similar to Asprey's. I intend purchasing a scarf of Persian silk. At least the assistants are French and know how to treat a customer with dignity.'

Their carriage rolled to a halt before an enormous pillared doorway with huge windows on either side of it. The coachman helped them to alight onto the broad pavement which had been cleared of snow, then Valerie followed Mrs Lees' majestic figure into the shop.

Inside, thick red carpets muffled every footfall and enormous chandeliers glittered overhead, almost as magnificent as those at the Winter Palace. They were as bright and sparkling as the diamond jewellery that nestled beneath on beds of black velvet.

For a moment Valerie gazed at the fabulous jewels and at the ornaments of jade and ivory, before following her companion past displays of umbrellas, walking sticks, and purses, to the area that displayed the scarves. These looked as colourful and fragile as a mass of butterflies' wings, stretched and festooned all over the stall.

Valerie had never been in such a shop before, nor seen such exotic items for sale, and she remained speechless with awe. Then a very elegant lady dressed all in black moved forward to greet them, speaking English with an attractive French accent.

'Whilst I am deciding on my scarf you take a look round, Valerie, and choose a little present for yourself,' said Mrs Lees. 'I don't suppose you are paid for all your time at the palace, are you, dear?'

'No,' said Valerie, turning her head away from the assistant's interested gaze and wishing that Mrs Lees wouldn't speak so loudly.

'Then go and look for a little something to take back to England as a keepsake, and I will pay for it, dear.'

How could she possibly find a 'little something' amongst all this finery? But Valerie thanked Mrs Lees and moved away to look at the stand of purses. Surely she could find something there that was not too extravagant to take home with her?

After studying some embroidered with gold and silver thread, some with sequins, and others of pigskin, suede, or velvet, she saw one of plain black suede, which would be most useful for her needs.

As Valerie was sighing with relief at having

59

found something suitable, she heard a familiar voice.

Raising her head with a jerk and staring across the stand of purses, she saw Pyotr deep in conversation with a very fashionably attired female. Their heads were bent as they stared down at the cases of jewellery, but Valerie knew at once who Pyotr's companion was.

She was so elegant in her narrow skirt and long, hip-length jacket of emerald green wool, that Valerie longed for the floor to open and drop her into oblivion in her dreary grey-blue coat.

Sophia's flower-pot hat was black, with a feather standing upright from the brim, and around her long neck was slung a sable wrap. Pyotr was wearing a long dark grey overcoat and black fur hat with his accustomed grace.

For a moment Valerie thought she was going to faint, but she forced herself to breathe deeply and recover her composure. Don't let Mrs Lees see them, she prayed, trying to hide herself away behind the purse stand. Let us take our purchases and get out of here!

But as she slowly retreated, moving back towards Mrs Lees with some object always between herself and the animated couple, the English woman's voice rang out, loud and carrying.

'Valerie, do look! There is your handsome count. We must go over and have a word with him. And who is his companion? Is she a member of the nobility? What a very stylish young woman.'

At the sound of her penetrating voice, Pyotr lifted his head and glanced across the floor.

'Who is that frightful woman?' whispered Sophia, watching as a large lady in maroon velvet bore down on them with a small, red-faced girl in tow.

'Mrs Lees.' Pyotr stepped forward to bow over the lady's outstretched hand. 'How very pleasant to see you again. And Miss Marsh.' He looked at Valerie, wishing she had worn a more becoming outfit. 'Have you been successful with your shopping?' he asked, with his charming smile.

'We were in the middle of our purchasing when I spotted you, dear count, and your exquisite companion,' crooned Mrs Lees. 'Do please introduce me.'

Sophia Lukaev nodded coolly, her eyebrows raised in surprise. Then she suddenly realized that the girl was the vision in white satin and pearls who had so alarmed her the night before.

'It is the birth day of Sophia's mother next week,' explained Pyotr, hoping Valerie would understand.

But she was turning away from his close scrutiny, and he knew he would have to deal with Miss Marsh with supreme delicacy if he were ever to gain possession of her tantalizing innocence.

At Mavara, he thought, would be the solitude and privacy so essential for court-ship, and she would be his. But first he had to make sure his Varinka would agree to visiting his estate.

Last night she had agreed wholeheartedly to his invitation, if the Empress gave permission. Today she looked as if she would gladly drive a dagger through his heart — if such a weapon were available at Alexandre's.

'We have decided on a brooch for Sophia's mother,' he said, but the English girl was walking away from him.

'I am going back to the purse stand,' she told Mrs Lees, interrupting the woman's lengthy chatter about what Mr Lees did, and what Mr Lees said, and perhaps Miss Lukaev used the bank where Mr Lees was installed?

'What, dear? Oh, very well, but hurry up, Valerie. As I have completed my shopping, perhaps Count Silakov and Miss Lukaev would care to join us for a little sustenance at the English Tea Room round the corner?'

Valerie marched away, determined to spend as much time as possible studying the purses.

She was *not* going to sit at a table and sip tea with that wretched man and his beautiful companion.

It was with great relief, therefore, that she heard Pyotr explaining that unfortunately they must decline the kind invitation.

Clamping her lips together, she waited for Mrs Lees to join her, as the count and Sophia left the shop. Never would she have anything more to do with that man. Thankfully anger made tears impossible. Sophia Lukaev was not the unimportant female Pyotr would have her believe, but too much wine, followed by that romantic sleigh-ride, had addled her wits last night.

'You don't have a fever, do you, dear?' said Mrs Lees, at her side. 'Your face is a most unbecoming red.'

'Only a bit hot,' said Valerie, adding quickly, 'but I do have a bit of a headache and would like to go home, when it suits you. I am sure a few hours on my bed will set me to rights.'

'Very well, then,' said the older woman, and led the way out of the shop.

She was annoyed by the disappearance of that delightful young man and his fashionable companion, and by her insipid little guest who didn't feel well.

It was no wonder Valerie had made a bad

impression on Count Silakov. Last night, in her satin gown and gleaming pearls she could have taken her place in Society and been an instant triumph. But this morning Valerie had appeared both gauche and plain beside the stunning beauty in emerald green, and Mrs Lees knew such a handsome and titled gentleman was never going to consider a badly-dressed sickly creature worth bothering about.

Valerie thought only of her quiet bedroom overlooking the river, where she could weep away her distress against the pillow.

'I will have that girl!' Pyotr strode up and down the sitting room in the apartment in Tsarskoe Selo. 'I love my little Varinka and she loves me — I know she does. But we have reached an impasse in our relationship and I am at my wits' end trying to think of a way to proceed with my courtship. She is small and fragile yet proving to be as stubborn as a mule.'

Andrei Odarka, stretching out his long legs, helped himself to another glass of vodka.

'Sit down, Petya, and think this out properly — like a battle campaign.'

'I have never been ignored before,' said Pyotr angrily, flinging himself down in the chair beside his friend and reaching for the bottle which stood on the table between them.

Neither ignored, nor refused, he thought, pouring a glass of the fiery liquid.

Many hearts had been broken in his tempestuous youth, but the young count had prided himself on being a courteous and generous lover, always making sure that small gifts and flowers were sent to console his admirers once the time came for them to part.

Now, for the first time, he desired a female who would not return his love. Yet the English girl was attracted to him, of that he was certain. She had proved it by her warm acceptance of his kisses during their sleigh-ride together.

Unfortunately, because of her stubborn pride, Valerie Marsh had turned her back on him and Pyotr did not know how to reclaim her affection.

'Why not beg Grand Duchess Olga to assist you in this affair of the heart?' said Andrei.

He was becoming bored by his friend's continual conversation about the foreigner and wished the pair would either sort out their differences or agree to part forever.

'Olga Nicolaievna?' Pyotr frowned. 'That is a possibility, my friend, for she has always been a caring young woman and she and Valerie are close companions. If she would only agree to coming with me to Mavara I know her heart could be won down there.'

'Whose?' said Andrei, with a grin. 'Olga Nicolaievna's?'

'No, you fool, my Little England's!'

'Then speak to Olga, but hurry up about it. Your leave is due next week, is it not?'

Glancing across at his friend's strong profile, Andrei believed that, as with all Pyotr's other conquests, this one would fade after a few weeks of bliss.

'I shall speak to the Empress,' said Pyotr suddenly, turning his head to smile at his companion, a devil lurking at the back of his eyes. 'I shall ask the Empress to aid me.'

Andrei stared in disbelief. 'How can she assist you in your immoral plan? Careful, Petya, lest you make a rod for your own back.'

But Pyotr was confident and filled with excitement. At last he knew what to do about the stubborn Miss Marsh.

'Empress Alexandra has always had a soft spot for me,' he said, 'because of my handsome face and manly figure. Haven't you noticed?' He leaned across to refill Andrei's empty glass. 'Drink this to my future, old friend, and to the conquest of that obstinate but oh, so desirable, Miss Marsh!' He raised his own glass and smiled again.

'What can the Empress do?' protested Andrei.

'I shall ask permission to take Valerie down with me to Mavara. I shall explain how much joy it will give my crippled sister to meet and talk to an English girl. And I am certain the Empress will agree.'

5

Mavara

As Valerie sat on the train carrying her and Dashka down to the Ukraine, she wondered if she had been outmanoevered. She had the strongest suspicion that Count Pyotr Silakov was in control once again. But she was determined to keep him at a distance when they next met at Mavara.

Pyotr had reserved a sleeping compartment for her, insisting on first-class travel, and had given her her railway ticket before he departed for his family home a few days earlier

Now Valerie watched as small villages flashed past the train windows, looking like splashes of brown and gold tapestry edged with white. Every now and again birch woods appeared with the trees' slender branches sparkling with frost and, occasionally, the high onion domes of distant churches decorated the skyline.

Apart from these fleeting glimpses of humanity there was an endless vision of snow. A white carpet on both sides of the track as the wide, flat steppes lay blanketed until the spring.

Although she was still angry with Pyotr, Valerie's talk with Empress Alexandra had helped to soften her attitude towards the young count.

The Empress had suggested that a visit to the Ukraine would be an interesting experience for her, and when Her Imperial Highness had also mentioned Tassya Silakov's name, and said she thought it would be a kindness on Valerie's part if she went and talked to the crippled girl, Valerie had been unable to refuse.

'You may well care to mention Our Friend's name,' the Empress had said, her dark blue eyes alight with trust. 'Father Grigorii is such a great healer he might be able to help Count Silakov's young sister, as he has been able to help our beloved son.'

There was no way Valerie could tell her that Pyotr was hopelessly prejudiced against the man from Siberia, so she had simply nodded at the Empress's words and remained silent. But if she could spend time with Tassya on her own, she might be able to plant a seed of hope in the girl's mind. That was another reason for accepting Pyotr's invitation.

For she had seen Father Grigorii again and

it had been such a heart-warming experience, that Valerie knew she, and the Imperial family, and Anna Vyrubova, were all right about the holy man and Count Pyotr Silakov completely wrong.

★　★　★

It had happened after the tsarevich fell awkwardly in his room, knocking his leg against the corner of a wooden cupboard. It was the first time Alexis had injured himself since Valerie had been at Alexander Palace, and she quickly learnt how appalling such a minor accident could be.

Within minutes the Empress had been informed. Olga and the other girls immediately joined their mother in the tsarevich's suite.

'You come too, Valerie,' Olga said, 'as we will not be able to concentrate on anything else until we have discovered how bad the injury is.'

The grand duchess's mouth was tight as she led Valerie along the passage to Alexis's rooms.

'If it is not too bad we can all return to our studies,' she said. 'But if Alexis has a bad attack then Tatiana and I will take it in turns to sit with him, just to give Mama a break.

She will never leave his bedside and sometimes his suffering lasts for days.'

The first room was filled with court officials, doctors, and the tsarevich's personal guard, as well as Anna Vyrubova. They were all talking in hushed voices, looking tense and worried.

In the bedroom beyond, the Empress sat beside her son's bed, wiping his brow with a damp cloth and talking quietly to him. Her left arm was around his shoulders, propping him against his pillows, and through the open doorway Valerie could see the boy's face blanched as white as his bed-linen, with dark patches beneath his eyes. He was moaning with pain and his body appeared twisted beneath the bed-covers.

'Can the doctors not do something?' she asked Tatiana, who had come in with her younger sisters as Olga went forward to join her mother.

Tatiana shook her head. 'There is nothing any of us can do except pray,' she said, falling to her knees beside Anna.

At that moment Tsar Nicholas strode in, pausing briefly to speak to the huddle of doctors by the door, then walking through to join his wife at the bedside.

Olga returned to kneel beside Valerie.

'It is very bad,' she whispered. 'Dr Fedorov

says the haemorrhage cannot be stopped and Alexis's temperature is rising.'

A tremor of fear shook Valerie's body. He wouldn't die, would he? But he was so young. Could nothing be done to save him?

She looked at the anxious faces all about her, particularly at the medical men. Surely they knew what to do? But they remained near the door talking and gesticulating in nervous undertones, as ineffectual as a cluster of crows.

'We should be used to these dreadful attacks,' said Olga, 'for Alexis seems to be having them more and more frequently.' She bit at her lower lip, trying to control her tears. 'I cannot believe that such a normally healthy boy could die, but it's the pain, Valerie. How much can such a young body endure?'

'Don't.' Valerie stretched out her hand and covered Olga's cold fingers with her own. 'Don't say any more.'

Her fingers tightened in Valerie's grasp as they both heard the piteous sounds coming from the other room.

'Help me, Mama: Help me!'

Forcing herself to look up, Valerie saw the Empress of all the Russias bending over her tortured son, murmuring words of comfort and love, trying to draw his pain into her own body.

That night, Olga, Tatiana, and Anna Vyrubova, took it in turns to stay by Empress Alexandra's side, endeavouring to make her have a few hours sleep. But Valerie and the two younger sisters were sent away — there was nothing they could do.

Then, some hours later, there was an urgent tapping on Valerie's door.

'Who is it?' She sat upright in the darkness, staring at the strip of yellow light that was framing her doorway.

'It is Anna,' called a soft breathless voice. 'Can you come, Valerie? Something wonderful has happened.'

When Valerie bade her enter, she came swiftly across to fling her arms around the English girl's neck, half-sobbing, half-laughing.

'It is Our Friend,' she said. 'The Empress sent for him just before midnight and he is here now. Come, dear, come and see what the man of God has done.'

Flinging her dressing gown around her, Valerie took Anna's hand and they ran together down the corridor that led to the tsarevich's apartment.

In the far chamber stood the dark-robed figure of Grigorii Rasputin. He was standing at the foot of the bed looking down at the boy. The Empress was sitting where she had been all day and night, her face pale and drawn with fatigue, but lit with a rare smile. And beside her Alexis slept, his body relaxed and colour beginning to return to his cheeks.

'The pain has gone,' said the Empress, glancing up. 'His fever has abated and my son sleeps.'

At the sound of her voice, Rasputin lifted his head and nodded.

'The little one is well again,' he said.

Then he turned and strode past Anna and Valerie, his black boots making no sound despite his solid build, a sheen of perspiration running down his face and into his beard.

'God does not hear my prayers, nor those of my family,' said the Empress softly. 'But His spirit rests upon Father Grigorii.'

Perhaps Father Grigorii would be able to help Tassya Silakov, thought Valerie, as the train puffed its way south. Her faith was as strong as the Imperial family's now and nothing Pyotr said would cause her belief to falter. Maybe she was being sent to Mavara as a messenger? Maybe God intended her to play a small part in Tassya's recovery?

Grand Duchess Olga had also encouraged the idea. Once she knew that her brother's life was out of danger, she had spent time with Valerie once more and was both intrigued and enthusiastic about the English girl's plans.

'You must bring her north,' she said. 'And we will make sure she meets Our Friend.'

Pyotr's heart gave a leap of joy as he stood on the platform of Kamenka railway station and saw his Little England alight.

There was no dull grey-blue wool today, but a dashing long coat of red fox fur with a matching hat, smart black button boots, and a black fur muff. Olga Nicolaievna had been at work again, he decided.

As he strode forward to greet her, her face lit up beneath the soft red fur, and his heart jumped again in triumph. Valerie Marsh was his now, and the thought of their passionate nights together at Mavara, filled him with almost drunken ecstasy.

'Varinka — you are here at last.' He bent to place his lips against her warm cheek, revelling again in the smooth, peachlike texture of her skin. 'I seem to have been waiting weeks for your arrival. I do hope the journey was not too long and tedious for you.' He took her case in one hand and placed the other on her arm. 'Come — the sleigh is waiting, ready to transport you back to my beloved Mavara.'

Valerie smiled up at him, unable to keep

her cool composure. Pyotr was so splendid in his wolfskin coat and fur hat, with his blue eyes dancing in his brown face. Due to so much riding his skin had a natural tan and she found him incredibly attractive. But she was not going to forget Sophia and would make sure she was never left alone with him.

In the station yard a sleigh was standing, drawn by two sturdy horses. The animals' breath was smoking through the frosty air as they stamped restlessly on the snow-covered earth, eager to be off. And the bells on their harnesses jingled and sparkled in the fading afternoon light.

'The journey was an interesting experience,' said Valerie, as Pyotr helped her into the sleigh and Dashka squeezed in beside her. Then he placed more furs around them before climbing in himself and gathering up the reins. 'Now I am looking forward to seeing your home, and meeting your mother and sister,' she said.

'Tassya is longing to meet you,' he said, as the sleigh began to move. 'Now, this is the main street of Kamenka, which is only a small village, as you can see, but we are very proud of our railway station. There are not many shops, but they provide us with all the necessities we cannot produce for ourselves.'

'Do you often visit Kiev?' asked Valerie,

looking from left to right as the shop windows lit up the white street.

'Very seldom,' said Pyotr. 'It is some 250km. from here and on the estate we live simple lives and manage to provide most of the everyday things.'

Once the lights of the village were left behind and the sky began to darken they had only the moon to guide them, but Pyotr knew the way well and told her the horses would find their way home even in a blizzard.

Across the snow-white carpet they skimmed, the only sound being the hissing of the runners beneath them and the cheerful tinkling of the little bells ahead.

'Over the next rise you will see the lights of Mavara,' said Pyotr, looking down at the girl who was snuggled warmly in her furs. It reminded him of the last time they had travelled together on a sleigh.

Valerie also remembered, and was thankful Pyotr was holding the reins and unable to put his arms around her. Life was so romantic in Russia with the sleigh-rides, and the snow, and the warm seductive furs. It was hard to keep a cool head in this fairy tale world beneath the silvery lustre of the moon.

But Mavara would be busy and noisy, bustling with life; there would be many people working and talking, hammering and cooking, cleaning and washing. She would have Tassya to talk to and would try to speak to her about the holy man and, although she would see Pyotr, she vowed he must never be allowed to overwhelm her with sweet words and tender caresses as he had done before.

'Here we are,' Pyotr said, slowing the horses as they entered a wide courtyard with the house looming ahead of them.

There were a great many outbuildings and the two unlit wings that reached out on either side of the yard, appeared hostile in the darkness.

But lights were shining cheerily from the main block and the front door was open, allowing lamplight to spill out onto the snow.

Pyotr drew the horses to a halt as a man-servant appeared in the doorway, calling out a greeting. As another man moved forward to take the reins, Pyotr helped Valerie from her furs and escorted her across the cleared path to be introduced to Feodor, with Dashka behind her.

Feodor was a short, ageless man without a wrinkle on his broad face. He possessed no hair on his pink scalp, but had a very bushy black beard and whiskers. He was attired in an old black frock coat, black trousers, and well-worn black shoes. Valerie liked the friendliness in his blue eyes and bulging cheeks when he smiled.

She followed Feodor into the hall, which was big and cold, with a tiled floor and wooden panels on the walls reaching up to the ceiling. Pyotr told Dashka to take Valerie's case to her bedchamber, then he led her through a door on the right, which opened into a spacious red-carpeted room. Here it was beautifully warm, and Valerie gave her outer garments to Feodor before moving forward and studying her surroundings.

A fire burned in the marble fireplace, and a round table stood in the middle of the room, covered with green felt over which was spread a white lace cloth. A samovar boiled happily on the table, surrounded by plates of fresh brioches, and buns, and a fruit cake.

It was pleasing to see a proper tea, after the plain biscuits at Alexander Palace, and Valerie was hungry. Several chairs were set around the table with green plush seats, and more well-worn armchairs were beside the fireplace and against the walls.

Suddenly a voice called out behind her.

'Petya — is she here?'

There was the sound of wheels in the hallway and Tassya arrived, her chair pushed by a maid-servant. Crouched low, Tassya's face was rosy with excitement beneath a mass of dark brown curls.

'Tassya, dearest sister, meet my very good friend, Valerie Marsh from England,' said Pyotr, as Valerie stepped forward to greet the girl.

To her astonishment, strong little arms were flung around her neck as Tassya reached up to hug her.

'I am so pleased to meet you, Miss Marsh. Please excuse my poor English. I try very hard to speak like you,' said Pyotr's sister.

Her eyes were blue, like her brother's, fringed with very dark lashes, and her hair was caught back at the sides but allowed to bounce in curls across her wide forehead.

Tassya looked younger than her 16 years, but her eyes were bright and intelligent and her English remarkably good.

'I am glad to meet you, Tassya, and please call me Valerie. I hope we'll become good companions during my short stay here.'

'I know we will,' said Tassya, 'and you must tell me all about England so I can picture it in my mind.'

When Valerie and Pyotr took their places at the table, Tassya was wheeled up to sit between them.

'Mother will be joining us soon,' she said, 'but she has some work in the study to finish, so please do not wait.'

Feodor moved around the table, handing

out the plates of brioches and buns, cutting the cake, then filling the cups of tea from the samovar. It was a relief to drink from delicate china cups after the long glasses at Alexander Palace, and Valerie ate and drank with relish. She felt agreeably comfortable in the company of Pyotr and his sister. Like being at home again, only warmer and cosier than the vicarage in Putney.

Countess Irina Silakov sat in her study with the desk strewn with papers, but her hands were still as she gazed blankly before her. She was unable to concentrate on anything other than the foreigner now in their midst.

How dare this girl come to Russia and steal her son's attention when he should be proposing marriage to Sophia Lukaev.

Sophia loved Pyotr, her parents liked him and, being so wealthy, would be sure to give their only child a magnificent dowry.

Ever since her husband had died, Irina had worked. She had forced herself to go to the big fair in Zlatopol to buy horses and oxen, and had become adept at trading and not being cheated.

Irina prided herself on her cattle, and had four pure-bred Swiss cows that had just begun breeding successfully. From the poorer stock she had managed to sell several calves to local peasants, who were at last becoming interested in the skills of agriculture.

The countess snorted to herself. She could remember the time when only the nobility could read and write, and enjoy literature and culture. But now even the moujiks were improving themselves.

They were growing beet in a more extensive way, improving the quality of their cattle, and even learning not to throw manure into the ditches but spread it on their fields instead.

However she, Countess Irina Silakov, remained in dire need of money. The barns, the enclosures, even the water troughs, needed repairing.

And what, thought Irina fiercely, could this English girl give her son apart from her lust-filled body?

The countess knew her Pyotr, knew from the look in his dancing eyes, from the tone of his deep voice, that this girl interested him far more than Sophia. But would she be content as his mistress? Or was she after his title? Irina knew the English were very fond of their lords and ladies, but that mistresses were frowned upon.

Bleakly she wondered how she could force herself to be polite to the intruder. Yet she dared not anger Pyotr and had promised to treat his guest with courtesy.

Slowly she rose to her feet. She could work no more this evening. There was too much confusion and bitterness churning in her mind. Now she must go and meet the unwanted guest.

As soon as Countess Irina entered the room and saw Valerie Marsh, she knew why Pyotr was attracted to her. The English girl was small and slender with brown hair held back in a soft bun, and with hands as white as her neck, which rose from the lace collar of her blue silk gown.

Everything about the girl reminded Irina of gentle, feminine meekness, and as she strode forward to grasp the little hand in her own hard, calloused one, she wanted to curse aloud.

How could Pyotr be such a fool as to show interest in this daughter of an English clergyman? What good would such a female be if ever he came back to run Mavara? It was inconceivable to imagine Valerie Marsh with a gun in her hands, with reins between her soft white fingers, or with the blood of an animal all over her skirts.

The beautiful Lukaev would also be of little use on the practical side but then *she* would not need to work. All Sophia would have to do would be spend money lavishly whenever it was needed.

'I am pleased to meet you, Miss Marsh,' said the countess, speaking stiffly in English as she took the chair next to her son. 'I hope you will not be bored at Mavara. Pyotr must spend much time with me, and Tassya will probably irritate you with her continual questions.'

She looked across at Valerie with eyes so dark they were almost black, and the girl realized that, despite her words, Pyotr's mother did not welcome her.

'I have explained to Valerie that you and I have much to do, Mother,' Pyotr said, smiling at the visitor and delighting in the faint blush, which stained her velvet-like skin. 'But she says she will be quite content to talk to Tassya and learn how we live out here on the estate.'

He knew which room had been made ready for her and, once the others were in bed — they all retired early at Mavara — he intended spending time with his Varinka and teaching her things far removed from the problems of the day-to-day life here.

'I am going to take Valerie all round our home tomorrow,' said Tassya, 'then we'll go into Kamenka. May we, Mother?'

'Whatever for?' The countess stared at her daughter, a frown creasing her brow. Her greying hair was scraped back into a tight bun and neither her wrinkled skin, nor worn black

84

dress, looked in any way aristocratic.

'We do not need anything from the shops this month, Tassya,' she went on, 'and every kopeck must be accounted for.'

'I will give her some money,' said Pyotr. 'Then she can buy herself a little gift, and perhaps Valerie would like a souvenir from her first visit to the Ukraine?'

Valerie remained silent, uncertain how to reply, as she saw the countess clamp her lips tightly together then hold out her cup for Feodor to fill.

But Tassya was clapping her hands in glee.

'Thank you, dear brother! It will be lovely having money to spend and I want Valerie to see our village in daylight.'

'It is not St Petersburg,' said Pyotr.

How he wished he could go with the girls and spoil them for a while. But he had to remain with his mother and endeavour to reassure her about the future.

'I shall enjoy seeing everything,' said Valerie, 'because it is all so new and different. And I won't be bored,' she added, glancing across at the countess.

But Irina was helping herself to a brioche and did not look up.

Valerie had been given a bedroom next to Tassya's on the ground floor, which was spartan in its furnishings and very cold. But the iron bed had plenty of woollen blankets on it, and Dashka brought her a bowl of hot water and a towel before she retired.

As she lay there, enjoying the feeling of warmth that was beginning to permeate her body, the door was quietly opened.

'Are you awake, Varinka?'

Lifting her head from the pillow and staring across at the lamplight that filled the room with its golden glow, Valerie saw Pyotr standing, a lamp held high in his right hand.

'May I come in?'

It was the last thing she wanted when she was so vulnerable in his presence, but she could scarcely shout out or cause a commotion in the quiet house.

'Come in quickly,' she whispered, propping herself up on one elbow and pushing back her loose, unbound hair with the other hand. 'And close the door.'

Pyotr grinned, shutting the door gently behind him then padding across towards her bed. He was wearing a loose wool jacket over his pale blue peasant-type blouse, and his feet were bare beneath his baggy trousers.

'My feet are cold,' he said, standing close to her bed and placing the lamp on the table beside her. 'May I sit with you, Little England, and warm them beneath your covers?'

With her heart beginning to pound she nodded, then struggled to an upright position and reached for her shawl.

'But keep your voice down — I don't want Tassya hearing us.'

Pyotr knew his sister would not interrupt them, but his mother was another matter. The countess often roamed around at night if she could not sleep, or if she felt like checking on the servants' nocturnal activities. But as both she and Pyotr slept upstairs, he had made sure there was no light beneath her door before venturing down.

'I have never seen you looking so like a little girl,' he said, sitting beside her with his back against the pillow and sliding his cold feet under the blankets. 'So young — and so fresh and innocent, my Varinka.'

Her small body was covered with a white flannel nightdress, very thick and totally unrevealing. Over this was slung a pink woolly shawl.

Valerie's shiny brown hair hung below her shoulders, silky smooth to his touch as he gave her a hug.

'You smell like an apple,' he said, nuzzling against her hair.

He wanted to kiss her cheeks and the tip of her nose, to cover her open breathless mouth with his own. Her lips were as red and luscious as the Crimean apples with which they decorated the tree at Christmas time.

But he must be patient. He dared not frighten his Varinka with sudden passion when he could tell, by the beating of her heart beneath the heavy flannel, that she was fearful and excited both at once.

'Why did you come here?' She was willing her body not to tremble. 'It was a foolish act, Pyotr. Say what you have to say and then go. I couldn't bear it if your mother found us like this.'

'Mother will not come,' said Pyotr, raising his hand and stroking back some of the curls that were tumbling across her brow. 'She is sound asleep upstairs.'

'Then what do you want to say to me?'

'I want to tell you that I love you and wish to continue with the joy we shared on our sleigh-ride through St Petersburg.'

He pressed his face against her hair again, nibbling at its satiny texture. But Valerie jerked away.

'I do not know what you mean by the word love, Pyotr Silakov,' she said. 'For me love means one man, forever, and no lying or cheating.'

'For me, also!' His dark eyebrows were raised in astonishment. 'That is what love is all about — one to one and complete honesty.'

'Then how do you explain Sophia Lukaev?'

'I have told you, Valerie, that she is unimportant. I do not love her but I *do* love you. Let me show you how much.'

He pulled her towards him placing both his hands around her face, lowering his own until their lips met. But he did not linger, kissing her but fleetingly before lifting his head and looking down at her again. His eyes were fierce in the lamplight as his thumbs caressed her cheeks.

'Come now, tell me what you have seen and heard about the Lukaev and me?'

'I have heard nothing,' she said, her limbs turning to water at his touch, 'but I am sure she loves you.'

'Maybe,' he said, laughing down at her, 'maybe she finds me as attractive as I find *you*, Little England.'

Then he kissed her again and this time his mouth stayed on hers, as firm and demanding, as in St Petersburg.

Valerie's resolve broke. She wanted to show, and share, the love she felt for this devastating man. With a moan of acceptance she lifted her arms and folded them around Pyotr's neck, as her shawl slipped to the floor.

Very gently Pyotr lowered one hand and began stroking her arching back, gathering up the folds of her nightgown and pulling the material up and up until his hands found warm flesh beneath.

Gasping, Valerie rubbed her body against his hand wanting him to touch her, fondle her, all over. Then her lips were on his ear and she was biting at the lobe before thrusting her tongue into the opening, making him cry out in delight.

When Pyotr reached to draw the nightgown up to her shoulders, she allowed him to tug it free then fling it away.

'I promised you,' he said. 'I promised we would share our love with nothing in the way.' His lips travelled down her throat, across one small perfect breast, then he ran his tongue over the hard little nipple, making her catch her breath in ecstasy. 'So small, so pure,' he said, fondling her other breast and bringing it, too, to a button-like erection.

'You too!' Perspiration was slithering down Valerie's body making everything hot and wet. 'Take your clothes off, Petya — I want to feel your body next to mine!'

Smiling, he raised himself to a kneeling position and pulled off his jacket, then his shirt. But at that moment came a tapping on the door and they both froze. There was not a sound in the chamber apart from the insistent tapping.

Then Valerie found her voice. 'Who is it?'

she croaked, as Pyotr rolled to one side and was on his feet in one deft, soundless motion. Valerie's throat was so dry she almost choked. 'Who is there?'

'It is Dunya,' came the voice of Tassya's maid-servant. 'My mistress heard you crying, bárishna, and says if it is bad dreams she also cannot sleep. Please to come.'

Recovering from her panic, Valerie looked at Pyotr.

'Go to her,' he mouthed.

'I'll come,' called Valerie. 'Tell her I'll come.'

Once her nightgown was back on and her air smoothed away from her radiant face, Pyotr kissed her briefly before placing the shawl about her shoulders.

'I shall leave after you have gone next door,' he said. 'Give Tassya all the time and sympathy she deserves, and we will have our joy another time, my heart.'

Valerie nodded before opening the door and going to join Pyotr's sister.

6

The following morning having breakfast at the big round table with Tassya, Valerie was relieved to find both Pyotr and his mother missing. They had eaten earlier and were already out on the estate.

But an attentive Feodor served the two girls freshly baked bread, butter, and apricot jam. 'All made here,' announced Tassya happily. There were also more cups of excellent tea from the bubbling samovar.

'It was so lovely when you came to my room last night,' she went on, 'and I am glad it was not a night-horse for you.'

'Nightmare,' said Valerie.

'I beg your pardon — nightmare. I have terrible dreams, filled with these mares and now it is nice knowing you are close to me.'

Valerie had spent almost an hour with Pyotr's sister the night before, thinking more than once that it must have been God's Will. He had saved her from Pyotr's compelling love-making and had also given her the chance to get to know Tassya better.

Pyotr said he loved her but did he mean lasting love? It was true that he was not engaged to Sophia, but there had been no words of marriage to Valerie, either, despite his ardent vows of affection.

If she were to give in to his demands, what then? Would he marry her? Would she become a countess and remain in Russia forever? Or would he tire of her once he had possessed her body and leave her heartbroken and alone?

Don't give in to him, she told herself grimly as she gazed across at Tassya's pretty face without really seeing it. Do *not* allow him to make love to you until his ring is on your finger. God had helped her last night, but she could not expect the Almighty to aid her every time she needed moral support.

She would have to exert her own self-discipline and keep a distance between herself and Pyotr, which was what she had intended doing when she first came down to Mavara.

If only she didn't love him. If only she didn't love him with a passion she hadn't known she possessed. Perhaps it was Russia. Perhaps it was this exotic, fascinating, glorious land in which she now dwelt. Valerie could not believe she would ever have been swept off her feet, almost drowning in an ecstasy of emotion, in the arms of some cleric in rain-sodden Putney.

But Pyotr Silakov, with his arrogance, self-confidence, and beauty, was a typical son of this vibrant land and his intense masculine vitality overwhelmed her.

'Valerie, I think you are far away,' said Tassya. 'You do not hear what I say to you.'

'Forgive me.' Valerie blinked, putting down her cup with a clatter. 'I am sorry, Tassya. I was thinking about Russia, and Mavara, and everything I have seen here. It is all so different and wonderful — my mind is reeling from the thrill of it all.'

'Reeling?' Tassya did not know that word.

'As if I have had too much vodka,' said Valerie, swaying from side to side on her chair, 'or like a ship on the high seas.'

She laughed, aware of how absurd she must look, but Feodor's face remained expressionless and Tassya nodded gravely.

'I do like you, Valerie Marsh, and wish you could stay for a longer time. I want you as my friend and do not wish you to go away so soon.'

'I must return to my duties with Grand Duchess Olga,' said Valerie. 'But I would love to come and visit again, if your mother agrees? Perhaps I could come in the summer?'

She was unsure what the Imperial family would be doing when they returned from the

Crimea after Easter. But the Empress was so sympathetic about Tassya, she might allow Valerie to come down again later in the year.

There was still the matter of Grigorii Rasputin to be sorted out. Valerie hadn't mentioned the holy man last night. Tassya had wanted to talk about her riding accident, and how she missed her adored horses, and how she hated being so dependent on other people.

Then Tassya had asked about England, and about Valerie's life at the vicarage, and by the time she had finished talking both girls were tired and ready for sleep.

The time had to be right before she dared to mention Father Grigorii and Valerie felt she needed to know Tassya better, in order to make sure she could keep a secret.

The girl worshipped her tall, goodlooking brother but she must not be allowed to speak about plans with the great healer to Pyotr. He would never let his sister make the long journey to St Petersburg if he suspected she was going to meet the man he detested.

'I am sure Mother would agree to you coming here again,' said Tassya, 'and *I* want you to look upon Mavara as your second home.'

'I should like that,' said Valerie.

'We have eight indoor servants,' Tassya

went on, enjoying herself now that Valerie was concentrating on her, 'four men and four women. They are really too many, but as I need Dunya all the time, that only leaves three for the cleaning and washing and ironing and sewing.'

'What about the cooking?' said Valerie.

Eight servants were far more than they had at home, where Mrs Duffy did all the work with just little Polly to help her. But the vicarage was tiny compared to Mavara, and there was a butcher's shop, and a greengrocer, just down the road.

'The cooking is done by Sidor Novatko, and even Feodor bows to his wishes in the kitchen, although Feodor is in charge of everything else in the house.' Tassya gave the black-clad man a fleeting smile as she spoke. 'Sidor Novatko has a boy to help with the wood for the stove, and for preparing the vegetables, and cleaning the silver. Our other man, Dimitry, is rather old and sleeps a lot, but he looks after the lamps.'

She went on to explain that Dunya slept with her, but the other three females slept upstairs next to her mother's bedroom, in the linen room.

'And where Dashka will be unless you want her with you at night?'

Valerie shook her head.

'It's so that Mother can hear if there is any nonsense,' she grinned.

'And the men all sleep downstairs,' Tassya went on. 'Feodor on a bed in the pantry, and the others on the kitchen floor.'

'Mrs Duffy wouldn't take kindly to sleeping on the floor!' said Valerie.

'But they have always slept like that.' Tassya sounded surprised. 'And they are fortunate in having proper meals every day and clothes provided by Mother. You should see how the moujiks live, Valerie.'

'Moujiks?' That was the name Pyotr had given to Father Grigorii.

'Moujiks are the real peasants,' said Tassya, 'who live in thatched huts with clay stoves and have too many children. They are all free now because we do not have serfs in Russia any more, but sometimes I think they were better off when they were owned. Especially if they had a kind master. During some bad winters I've seen them begging all through Kamenka and it's a horrid sight,' she said sadly.

'Can you not help them?' said Valerie.

There was poverty in England, too, and during the winter months Valerie and Mrs Duffy ran a soup kitchen, organized by her father.

'Help them?' said Tassya, her eyes wide.

'How can we, when there is famine and we are in trouble ourselves? Anyway, Mother says if they will have so many children, and if they won't look after their land properly, it is their own fault if they starve. There are hundreds and hundreds of moujiks, Valerie. We couldn't possibly feed them all.'

Surely Mavara, with its vast lands, could give something to the poor in times of disaster? Wasn't there game in the wooded areas, and timber for fires? But it was no good arguing with Tassya, who had problems enough of her own, so Valerie changed the subject.

'As soon as we have finished breakfast you must show me around. I am longing to see Mavara in daylight.'

Tassya's face brightened. 'I will show my English friend everything. Dunya, call for Conrad to come — we are going out.'

Once the girls had put on their warm outer garments, they joined Conrad in the hall. He was a big burly man with a wide Slavic face and a cheery grin. He lifted Tassya's chair with ease down the steps and out into the yard. Then the tour of inspection began along the snow-shovelled paths.

'This is my favourite place,' said Tassya, 'and Manya, the baker woman, will give us a piece of her plum cake to take on our drive to

Kamenka this afternoon.'

She explained that Sidor Novatko did not attempt to make bread or any cakes or biscuits. His task was to prepare proper meals for the household.

Valerie thought the bakery would be her favourite place, too. It was a big, high-ceilinged room with tall windows overlooking the yard, and a tantalizing smell of vanilla and cinnamon adding to that of newly baked bread. On a table near the door was an array of jars filled with many different jams.

'Manya makes all our jams, as well,' said Tassya, as Dunya rolled her chair forward to greet the large smiling baker woman, who was kneading dough at another table.

After that visit, with two good slices of plum cake wrapped in a white cloth ready for their afternoon's expedition, Valerie followed Tassya to the hammam.

Tassya couldn't think of a word to translate this, neither could Valerie, but she supposed it was a kind of bath-house. An enormous boiler filled one corner of the large room and rows of wooden shelves lined the opposite wall.

'We have two bathrooms in the house,' Tassya said, 'but we come here on a Saturday evening, which is the proper time for the hammam.'

'What are those shelves for?'

Tassya gave a contented sigh.

'On Saturday afternoon the boiler is lit underneath and filled with water. Slowly the steam rises and the room gets lovely and hot. Mother and I have our hair washed, and then Dunya washes my body and I lie on one of those shelves covered with a towel and feel really content. Mother does the same.'

'It must be good to have that warmth, and I'm sure your mother must benefit after all her hard work. But doesn't it get too hot, sometimes?'

Valerie didn't think she would like to be shut in a room full of steam.

'No, but it is best in winter when the snow is all over the yard and we come into this wonderful warmth.' Tassya paused. 'In the summer we used to go down to the lake,' she said, 'but I can't do that now and Petya is away so much, and Mother is too busy, so our lovely picnics have stopped.'

If Tassya could meet Father Grigorii, and if he could help her, perhaps she would be going down to the lake next year?

Sighing, Valerie followed Dunya as she pushed the chair back towards the house.

'Hurry,' called Tassya, as the English girl's footsteps dragged behind her, 'we must go and prepare ourselves as Conrad will have the troika ready by noon. We go to Kamenka early as it gets dark so quickly these days.'

* * *

Just before setting off for Kamenka, Valerie saw Pyotr again.

'May I come in?' he called softly, knocking at her bedroom door.

As she went to open it she was already wearing her red fox fur coat and matching hat.

'Are you happy, Little England?' He closed the door behind him and reached out for her. 'Are you enjoying your first visit to Mavara?'

Valerie nodded, placing her hands on his chest. 'I am enjoying it very much and Tassya and I are just off to Kamenka. But last night was a mistake, Pyotr. You must not come to my room again.' Giving a little push she stepped back from him.

'Not come? But when can I see you — talk to you alone? It is impossible to tell you what is in my heart when my mother and sister are always present.' She couldn't deny him — not after the unfolding passion of last night. She couldn't refuse to see him when Mavara was the only place they could be alone together — the place where they could share their love for the first time. 'Tassya did not hear us? She does not suspect?'

'No, but — '

'Then it is quite safe for me to come to you, Varinka and I shall come again tonight. But perhaps a little later — once we are sure that Tassya sleeps.'

He reached for her again, but Valerie retreated, shaking her head. There was no lock to her door, nor bolt, but she would pull her bed across to block his entry. She *had* to remain strong, had to remember that she was a clergyman's daughter and brought up to remain pure until marriage.

And there was still the shadow of Sophia, despite Pyotr's denials.

'Pyotr, you have got to understand,' she said. 'You invited me to Mavara to see your home, and to meet Tassya. I came as your friend, not your lover, as I am sure Empress Alexandra intended. Neither she, nor my father, would look kindly on your behaviour.'

She had to convince him, had to make him see what was in her mind, if not her heart. But Pyotr would not listen.

'That was not the way you felt last night,' he said. 'You love me, Varinka, you know you do. And I have only to take you in my arms again and you will give in.'

She knew she would. That was the reason there must always be space between them and no more nocturnal visits.

'Valerie, are you ready? The troika is ready and Conrad has come for me. Please make haste, my friend.'

Pyotr started at the sound of Tassya's voice, and Valerie was able to pass him and open the door.

'I'm coming!' she called, then looked back into the room. 'Don't spoil these days, Pyotr. Let us enjoy them calmly and with friendship. I am so grateful for your invitation, but I mean it about tonight.' She looked across at him with steady eyes. 'Do not waste time in coming — I shall not change my mind.'

With a muffled curse, Pyotr strode out behind her, as she went to join Tassya and he went to join his mother in the study. There was still much paperwork to be sorted out, though whether he could concentrate with his thoughts in turmoil, he didn't know.

Valerie loved him. He knew she did. So why was she playing this prim-and-proper role? Did she hope to trick him into marriage? Of course such a move was quite impossible, but before being totally committed to Sophia, he wished for a few months of happiness with his Varinka.

★ ★ ★

When the two girls set off in the troika, which was larger than a sleigh and drawn by three horses, they carried with them the precious kopecks that Pyotr had given them.

It was just as well they had received the coins earlier, thought Valerie. He might not have been so generous to her after their recent encounter. She felt miserable about hurting him, but he had to realize that she would not become his mistress.

Forcing herself to concentrate on what Tassya was saying, she turned her head to listen as the girl prattled on. Dunya was not with them as there was no room for a fourth person, and both Conrad and Valerie could assist Tassya.

'They are all Jewish shops in Kamenka and the Jews sell everything,' she was saying. 'What do you want to buy, Valerie?'

Valerie pondered. There was nothing she really wanted for herself and little point in taking anything back for Olga. The Imperial family possessed everything money could buy — apart from freedom and good health for the tsarevich.

'I can't think of anything at the moment,' she said. 'What about you, Tassya?'

'Paper and envelopes,' said the girl. 'So I can write to you when you go away.'

Valerie smiled. 'And I promise to answer

every letter,' she said.

'Will you really? Then I shan't feel that you have gone so very far away,' said Tassya softly.

It would be a pleasing form of contact for both of them, but particularly for Tassya, with her lonely life stuck in the wheelchair. However, Valerie's heart lifted in hope, perhaps quite soon they would meet again in St Petersburg.

Maybe this evening, if Tassya were not too weary, maybe she could go next door and tell her about the miraculous powers of Grigorii Rasputin?

★   ★   ★

When they reached the main street of the village, Conrad carried Tassya and her chair over the snow and into one of the small, single-storeyed shops. Valerie followed, her eyes roaming all over the items for sale. She intended giving Pyotr's sister her writing paper, but hoped for something extra, as well. She wanted some little gift with which to surprise her.

After studying the soap and bottles of perfume, the pencils and crockery, the candles and lamp-holders, all jammed together on the shelves, she saw what she wanted. She stepped away from Tassya, who was busy bartering with the Jewish shopkeeper, and touched Conrad's arm.

It would be easier to deal with him than with a stranger, and Valerie's Russian was still very shaky.

After showing Conrad how many kopecks she had, Valerie pointed at the bottles of perfume then put her finger to her lips and nodded in Tassya's direction. The big man understood and beamed at her before speaking to the second attendant. At once several bottles were brought out for her inspection.

Unfortunately, the price of that plus the writing paper and envelopes, was more than she could afford. But with much shaking of her head and showing the amount in her hand, and with Conrad's bearlike figure looming over them, Valerie managed to purchase all three items.

Luckily Tassya had surprises of her own and was not curious about Valerie's shopping.

'I have bought you something special for when you go away,' she said, clutching a small paper bag on her lap. 'But you are not to see it until you leave Mavara.'

'Then I will give you mine at the same time,' said Valerie, 'and it will be like Christmas!'

As they left the shop it was already turning

dark and there was a bitter wind blowing down the street. Conrad lifted Tassya's chair onto the troika, then handed both girls extra furs to place around their knees and shoulders. Then he clambered up in front and called to the horses to make for home.

'It's going to snow again,' said Tassya, sniffing the air. 'I hope we have a blizzard and get snowed in. Then you won't be able to leave us.'

Valerie smiled at the bright face beside her, thankful for the extra furs and for the warm coat Olga had given her. Winters in Russia were far colder and fiercer than English ones, and her grey wool coat would have been useless in these icy temperatures.

Perhaps the wind was blowing all the way from the Siberian wastes, she thought, and was about to bring up the subject of Grigorii Rasputin, when Tassya interrupted her.

'If we were snowed in for days Pyotr would fall in love with you and forget all about Sophia Lukaev,' she said.

'Has Sophia been to Mavara?'

'Only once, but her visit seemed to last for ages. Her parents were with her and Mother was all silly and trying too hard to please,' said Tassya. 'It was most embarrassing.'

'I am surprised they didn't announce their engagement then,' said Valerie, with a sick feeling in her heart.

'Pyotr is awfully stubborn and won't be pushed,' said his sister. 'The more Mother, and Sophia, and her parents, tried to please him the colder he became. Mother was very cross with him after they'd gone.'

'If they are not engaged what makes you think she will become his wife?'

'Because I heard Mother telling him he *must* propose to Sophia this year or she'll have to sell Mavara.'

So that was that. For the rest of the drive both girls were silent, immersed in their own thoughts. But as the troika reached Mavara and turned in between the iron gates, Tassya let out a gasp.

'We've got visitors!'

She leaned forward in her chair and stared at the brightly lit forecourt.

Two sleighs were drawn up by the front steps, one empty the other being unloaded by a tall man in a long fur coat and fur hat, and a harassed looking Feodor.

'Who can it be? We never have visitors. Is it a friend of Pyotr's?'

As Conrad halted the troika and jumped down to lift out Tassya's chair, the tall man came down the steps and called out a greeting.

'Good evening, Tassya, remember me?'

'It's Andrei!' cried Tassya. 'Hurry, Conrad, get me into the house! It's Andrei Odarka, Valerie,' she called back over her shoulder, as Conrad carried the chair up the steps.

'I remember him,' said Valerie, following them into the house.

In the hallway Pyotr was waiting, concern on his lean face.

'You are late!' he said, his blue eyes dark with annoyance. 'Mother is in a dreadful state with these unexpected guests and you were not here to welcome them.' He glared at Valerie as if it was her fault.

'We are back now so your mother needn't worry,' she said.

'And it was such fun spending your money, dear brother, thank you for being so generous,' said Tassya, smiling up at him.

But Pyotr was not appeased.

'Go and change for dinner,' he snapped. 'Dunya is waiting in your room.'

He did not look at Valerie again, but strode past her to the door and began shouting orders to Conrad about the horses.

'Sorry to have caused you stress,' said Andrei, following his friend back into the hall, with Feodor close on his heels. 'There, that's the lot now. I'll take these up to Sophia and then join you for a drink, Petya.'

After Andrei had left the hall, Pyotr was

further annoyed to see the two girls still sorting out their purchases.

'Take Tassya to her room, Valerie,' he said brusquely, 'then come and join us in the drawing room when you are ready.'

What a shattering day it had been. As he watched the English girl wheel his sister away down the passage, her back ramrod straight, he decided he needed a drink before Andrei came to join him.

First there had been the maddening behaviour of Valerie Marsh refusing to see him in her room that night. Then he and his mother had spent hours over the books in her study, making him realize just how bad the financial problems at Mavara really were.

Then Tassya and Valerie had been late returning and when horses did eventually arrive, they had been drawing sleighs carrying Andrei and Sophia with enough luggage for a fortnight's stay.

His mother was now having to organize meals for two extra and unwelcome guests, as well as having fires lit in the normally unheated spare bedrooms, and sorting out blankets and linen for the unaired beds.

After filling a glass of vodka, Pyotr slumped in his chair stretching out his legs and drinking lustily.

Sophie had been to Mavara before with her

parents, but that had been in the summer, his mother had been warned in advance, and in the warmth of a golden July life on the estate had been tranquil and relaxed.

He remembered picnics down by the lake, meals eaten out-of-doors on the verandah overlooking the garden at the rear of the house, and his mother liking both Sophia and her parents.

Now everything had changed. Pyotr tilted his glass and finished the vodka with one jerk of his hand. Now Valerie Marsh had entered his life and, despite their disagreements and her refusal to comply with his wishes, he could not erase her from his mind, nor from his future.

He would have to marry Sophia Lukaev. There was no doubt about that. But he was not prepared to let his Little England go. She tantalized, irritated, and enchanted him, and he had somehow to use all his wits and charm into persuading her to be his mistress.

Slowly Pyotr re-filled his glass and began to feel better.

★ ★ ★

Valerie wheeled the excited Tassya to her room and left her in Dunya's capable hands before returning to her own chamber where

111

Dashka awaited her.

At least she had garments that she could wear with pride, thanks to Grand Duchess Olga, and she had Dashka to assist her. But Valerie did not believe the maid would be able to style her hair the way she wished it.

So she gave Dashka her fur and blue travelling suit to deal with and slipped on her long-sleeved cream peignoir. Then she sat on the stool in front of the mirror and turned her attention to her hair. Once that was arranged to her satisfaction, Dashka could help her with the apple-green satin dress.

Heaving a sigh of determination, Valerie began undoing the pins and combs that kept her bun in place, then brushed out her long tresses until they shone like silk in the lamplight. The back locks returned to their normal bun and were coiled neatly at the back of her head. But the shorter side curls were not going to be pinned back from her face as usual.

Instead, she fumbled in the small drawer in front of her and brought out the two side-pads, which she had brought with her from Tsarskoe Selo. Then with her tongue caught between her teeth, she began folding the loose curls over the pads, one to the right the other to the left, before anchoring them firmly with the grand duchess's gold-encrusted combs.

Once she had finished, Valerie smiled. The style gave width to her small face, as well as elegance, and with a thick gold necklace around her throat she looked almost regal.

Dashka helped her with the dress then, with velvet slippers on her feet, Valerie stood for the last time in front of the long mirror.

Her bodice and sleeves were of tucked white lace, caught at the wrists and neck with tiny pearl buttons, and over the rest of her slithered the apple-green satin. This had a high waist seam and was buttoned down to the hem, ending in narrow flared skirts, which allowed freedom of movement.

After Dashka had given her the green and white lace fan, Valerie moved towards the door feeling taller and more confident. She didn't know if her attire was correct for Mavara, but she was certain it would compare favourably with anything Sophia was wearing.

As she opened her bedroom door she heard scurrying footsteps and Dunya, very red in the face, came to a breathless halt in front of her.

'They are waiting for you, bárishna,' she said.

'I am coming.' Valerie took a deep breath and followed Dunya down the passage.

★　★　★

Countess Irina was the first to see Valerie. She was sitting in her chair facing the door, prepared to make an immediate critical comment on the foreigner's late arrival. She had been watching and waiting, determined to put the English girl at a disadvantage and prove to her son, once and for all, that the clergyman's daughter was not right for Mavara and certainly not the right sort of female to become his wife.

But as she opened her mouth to speak, Countess Irina was stunned into silence.

The girl radiated unusual beauty with her brown hair puffed out at the sides and ornamented with combs of gold. She had the appearance of nobility with her graceful satin-clad figure and thin-wristed hands, one of which was playing delicately with her fan.

If Valerie Marsh were not a foreigner, and if her family had possessed reasonable wealth, she would have made an admirable bride for Pyotr, thought Irina, as her earlier views were dashed by the apparition in the doorway.

Sophia was the next to see her. The men were immersed in conversation at the other end of the room, and Tassya had her back to the door and was watching Andrei Odarka.

Sophia stared. The foreign upstart had done it again, she thought indignantly. But where had she obtained such a divine creation? It was a superbly cut garment with exquisite detail and finish. Had she brought it with her from England?

Furtively, her eyes slid round to look across at Pyotr. What effect would this ravishing creature have on him?

At that moment Andrei caught sight of Valerie over his friend's shoulder, and he stopped talking at once to gesture towards the door.

'Miss Marsh has arrived, Petya,' he said, 'and I think we must compliment her on her magnificent appearance.'

He looked at his friend. How would Pyotr react? He was half in love with the girl already, and in that stunning outfit she seemed born to be a countess, at the very least.

Pyotr spun round to stare at the open doorway where Valerie still hovered, unsure whether to come in and join the group, or whether they would all now rise and go through to the dining room.

He had still not recovered from her words of dismissal, nor from the unexpected arrival of Sophia. Moreover, the St Petersburg beauty he could have at any time, but did not desire, and the one he lusted after refused his love.

To make matters worse, here she was looking like an elegant, sophisticated society lady, when all he wanted was his innocent, simply dressed Little England.

He might poke fun at her lack of fashion, and turn up his nose at her dowdiness, but beneath the mockery was his longing to protect and cherish such naiveté.

Tonight, Valerie Marsh looked supremely confident and he hated the pride he detected in her, a pride that was one of his own worst failings.

'Valerie,' he said smoothly, 'how nice you look, my dear. No doubt such careful grooming made you late. Shall we eat now, Mother?' He offered his arm to the countess. 'I am famished,' he said, and led his mother past Valerie and out of the room.

Silently Valerie watched, as first Pyotr and his mother, then Andrei and Sophia, went past her.

'You look lovely, Valerie,' said Tassya's warm little voice, as Dunya wheeled her forward, 'like a real princess'.

She slipped her hand into the English girl's, knowing her brother had not been kind and wanting to console her.

'You look more beautiful than Sophia

116

tonight and I am sure she is wishing she looked like you, and Pyotr is wishing you had her money.'

Valerie smiled down at her companion, but didn't speak as they moved along the corridor in the direction of the big, seldom used, dining room.

It was very foolish to have dressed in such a grand manner to try to compete with Sophia. Tomorrow she would go back to being herself and concentrate on Tassya, and trying to persuade her to travel north to meet Father Grigorii.

That was the most important thing now. Not attempting to impress Count Pyotr Silakov and his mother.

7

All through the meal Sophia dominated the conversation, determined to have everyone's attention.

Whilst Valerie strove to enjoy the servings of fish and salted cucumbers, goose with apples, and marinated fruits, Sophia chattered and laughed, fluttering her lashes and tossing her head first at Pyotr, then at Andrei.

The countess did not speak at all and merely pecked at the various dishes, but Tassya finished everything Feodor set before her then looked around for more.

Valerie smiled at the young girl's healthy appetite, but had difficulty in enjoying the small amounts she put in her mouth. However, she drank as much of the wine as she could and hoped it would help her through that painful evening.

Perhaps Pyotr would find solace with Sophia tonight? Valerie was sure the beauty would not refuse him, and was equally sure that his mother would approve of *that* relationship. All Valerie wanted was to leave Mavara as soon as possible and return to the family who really cared for her.

When the meal was completed they all moved to another room, a big salon at the rear of the house where Valerie had not been before. It must have been used for dances in the old days for the wooden floorboards were bare, there was a dusty grand piano in the far corner, and many high-backed chairs and one old brown sofa were set against the walls.

A fire was burning in the open grate warming the room with its glow, and an oil lamp on the piano added its light to the stark surroundings.

'You must come and stay with us in St Petersburg, dear Tassya,' said Sophia suddenly, turning towards Pyotr's sister. 'I should love to spoil you for a while.'

They had all taken their places on the various chairs, with Sophia and Andrei on the sofa, and Tassya's chair wheeled up close to Valerie's.

'You are very kind.' Tassya's face was bright pink. 'But I don't feel able to manage such a long journey.'

'Perhaps, if Miss Marsh were to ask Grand Duchess Olga very nicely, the Imperial train could be sent to bring you to the capital,' said Andrei, with a wink at Valerie.

Although he had not thought much of the English girl previously, she had astonished him tonight; much as she had surprised him that night at the Winter Palace. He did not feel Pyotr was treating her kindly this evening when she was looking so stunning.

'No doubt Valerie Marsh could get the Imperial train for you,' agreed Sophia silkily. 'She seems able to get everything she wants in Russia, even though she is a foreigner.'

'The Tsar likes foreigners,' put in Countess Irina. 'He even married a German woman — though what good she has done our beloved country, I do not know, producing four daughters and then an imbecile son.'

'Now, Mother,' broke in Pyotr swiftly, 'the tsarevich is not insane, you know that quite well.'

'Then why is he not seen more often in public? Why is he frequently ill? And why, when he does appear on some grand occasion is he often carried in the arms of his bodyguard? I have seen the photographs.'

Valerie clasped her hands together, wishing they could be told the truth. Then there would be sympathy for the Imperial family instead of these unpleasant and misleading guesses.

'Maybe Tsarevich Alexis has also suffered from an accident?' said Tassya. 'Being heir to the throne, it must be awful for him if he is in pain. Still, I've heard that the Romanovs are most devoted to each other — so that must be a great help in times of sorrow.'

Pyotr stood up and went across to stand beside his sister.

'And you have *our* love and devotion, Tassya, don't ever forget that,' he said, placing one hand on her narrow shoulder and looking down at her with a tenderness not often seen on his face.

Valerie felt close to tears. How she longed to be part of the Silakov family. Even though Irina looked like a witch in her black crêpe, with her greying hair scraped back into a tight bun and her hard-working hands for once lying still on her lap, Valerie longed to help her. Hard work had never bothered her and she knew there was much she could do at Mavara.

However, the invitation to Tassya to visit St Petersburg was a welcome possibility. If the girl would agree to staying with the Lukaevs, it would help Valerie's plan enormously. She felt quite cheerful until Sophia spoke again.

'I want to know why that peasant, Grigorii Rasputin, spends so much time over at Tsarskoe Selo,' she said, intent upon drawing attention back to herself. 'Some say he goes to pray over the tsarevich when he is ill. But others insist he spends most of his time with the Empress in her mauve boudoir. What do *you* think, Valerie Marsh? Ladies are wild about him in Petersburg, and I've heard he's not only a man of God, but also a very fine man of the flesh!'

Valerie's face reddened. How dare that spoilt female say such things about the great healer!

If only she could tell them about Alexis's terrible bleeding and how Grigorii Rasputin was the only person who could help him. Pyotr knew of the boy's suffering, but he didn't know how he had been saved. If she could tell them it would prove Father Grigorii's true worth.

'Yes, I have had the honour of meeting Father Grigorii,' she said, 'and found him a most sincere and pious man.'

'Pious!' exclaimed Sophia. 'That is scarcely what *I* have heard. Although he endeavours to cleanse people of their sins they have to sin first — and preferably with him!' She glanced at Pyotr, her eyes alight with mischief. 'Would you mind if I sinned with the Siberian moujik, Petya? Would that make you jealous?'

Pyotr, irritated by talk of the peasant and knowing of Valerie's interest in the man, left his sister's side and walked over to the piano.

'If you feel compelled to sin with Rasputin, why should it disturb me, Sophia? Do as you wish, dear lady. Now let us change the subject and allow beauty to dominate the rest of this night.' He lifted the piano lid and looked across at the girl in primrose velvet. 'Play for us, Sophia, and use your gift of music to lighten our hearts, I beg.'

When she stopped playing there was silence in the room apart from muffled sobs coming from Tassya, whose head was bent forward as she tried to control her tears.

'Was my playing so depressing that you had to weep, Tassya?' asked Sophia gently.

'It was so beautiful I could not help myself,' cried the girl. 'You made me cry from joy, Sophia Lukaev!'

That broke the spell and everyone laughed and clapped, and exclamations of congratulations flew around the room, pleasing the pianist and making Valerie realize that Sophia was very talented as well as beautiful.

'If you love music, Tassya, you must make the effort to visit St Petersburg,' said Sophia, swinging round on the stool. 'I will take you to the Mariansky Theatre where we will watch Karsavina dance, and to the opera to hear Fedor Chaliapin sing. And you will love it all, I know you will!'

She leaned forward, a soft graceful figure in her yellow gown.

'Just say you will come, Tassya, and you'll have a wonderful time.'

Tassya frowned. 'Will Valerie be there?' she said.

Sophia hesitated but before she could think of something to say, Valerie broke in.

'Why not come with us when we return to St Petersburg?' she said. 'I shall be going down to the Crimea with the Imperial family for Easter, but until then I shall be at Tsarskoe Selo. It would be lovely to see you again. Oh, please come, Tassya.'

Fortunately Andrei came to her aid. 'Let us decide now on Tassya Silakov's triumphant entry to the capital,' he announced, standing up and moving to the centre of the room, 'and celebrate accordingly!'

'But I am not sure.' Tassya looked across at her mother. 'Would it be all right to go?' Then she looked at Sophia. 'Are you sure your parents will not mind a girl in a wheelchair in their house? Oh, Valerie, I would love to travel with you and Petya when you go north. And perhaps I could meet Grand Duchess Olga? I can't believe all this could really happen to me.' She was almost crying again.

'You go with them,' said Countess Irina gruffly. 'It will be the only chance you will ever have of making that long journey. So, if Sophia means it, you have my blessing.'

'Of course I mean it!' said Sophia. If Tassya was a guest in her home it would mean more visits from her handsome brother to the Lukaev mansion.

Pyotr did not comment. It would be good for his sister and future bride to get to know each other better, but he did not intend proposing to Sophia just yet. First he had to sort out matters with the difficult Miss Marsh.

'That is settled then,' said Andrei, with a grin at the ecstatic Tassya. 'Now play us a waltz, Sophia, a waltz by Chopin, and I shall take great pleasure in dancing with you, Tassya Silakov.'

Sophia, glancing at the tall fair-haired man who was about to lift a gasping, squealing girl up in his strong arms, smiled and turned back to the piano.

As the light joyous sound floated into the sombre room, Andrei moved with it holding Tassya like thistledown, his body swaying in time to the melody.

Tassya's poor wasted legs were hidden beneath the folds of her scarlet dress and with one arm around Andrei's neck, the other on his chest, she looked happier than Valerie had ever seen her.

That was how she should always look and, maybe, with Father Grigorii's help, a normal life lay ahead for the young girl. A life where she could walk, and dance, and flirt, to her heart's content.

Suddenly her thoughts were broken by Pyotr's voice.

'Miss Marsh, may I have the pleasure?'

He had ignored her for long enough and now was the perfect time to put his arms around her and show forgiveness. Besides, he loved dancing and had learnt at the Winter Palace what an excellent partner his Little England was.

Valerie was caught unawares. But the music, and Tassya's happiness, lulled her into submission.

'Thank you, Count Silakov,' she replied, with equal formality.

He placed one hand around her waist and caught her right one in his firm grasp, then they were close, as close as they had been at the Grand Ball. As they moved in unison to the haunting notes of the music, Valerie relaxed.

'Well, Varinka, how are you feeling?' His voice was low, his lips almost touching her hair. 'This is right, is it not? Our bodies almost as one.'

She tried to pull back a little, aware of his thighs brushing against the clinging satin of her gown, of his wine-scented breath against her cheek.

'Don't hold me so close,' she whispered, wishing she didn't love him, wishing she

126

didn't care about Sophia.

'Tonight,' he said. 'Do not bar your door tonight, my love.'

She was shaking her head and stepping back, as Sophia brought her hands down on the keys with a thump.

'I have had enough of this!' she cried. 'It is all very well for me to play for you, but where is the enjoyment for *me*?'

She left the piano and walked across to face Pyotr, ignoring Valerie.

'If your sister is to travel with us there is much to arrange before our departure. May I have your attention now? Or do you intend spending the rest of this evening with the foreigner?'

'My time is yours, Sophia,' said Pyotr smoothly, as Valerie went to join Tassya.

The countess was glaring at him and both Andrei and Tassya appeared shocked by the strength of Sophia's outburst.

'Don't take any notice,' whispered Tassya, as Valerie sat on the chair beside her. 'She's only jealous because of your friendship with my brother.'

Valerie nodded, but didn't say anything as Pyotr sought to calm The Lukaev.

'I'm sorry you didn't have the chance to dance, but who else has your talent for making music, Sophia? And if I was holding

Valerie Marsh a little too close, it was simply to punish you, my dear, for your comments about Rasputin.

'Do not imagine that you are the only one to feel the twinges of jealousy, beautiful Sophia.' He reached out to take her hands as he gazed steadily into her indignant face.

'So you *would* mind if I sinned with that Siberian lecher?'

'I would mind very much if your lovely body was despoiled by that peasant. Now, come with me and let us drink wine together and plan for the exciting journey we are soon to undertake, with my sister.'

Pyotr placed her hand on his arm, smiled across at Tassya, then moved away to pull the bell-cord by the fireplace.

'I shall ask Feodor to bring us refreshments in the library. Please excuse us, Mother.'

He bowed to the countess, who was blinking like an owl in the lamplight, unsure how the evening's entertainment had ended.

Was Pyotr sincere in his affection for Sophia? Then what of the English girl, with whom he seemed even more enamoured? What was going on in her family?

Countess Irina wished she had not drunk so much wine, which hadn't agreed with her. Her head was thick and fuddled, she did not feel well, and would have to rise early in the morning as usual.

'Do as you please,' she said abruptly, getting to her feet. 'I am off to bed and intend getting some sleep before tomorrow.'

Andrei rose as well and bowed to the countess before turning to the two seated girls.

'How about a drink before we make for our beds? Valerie, Tassya, will you join me whilst the others make preparations for our journey north?'

Pyotr handled that well, Andrei thought with relief; he knew how his friend felt about both Sophia and Valerie Marsh and, being a quiet, easy-going man, he had dreaded a scene in the antiquated ballroom at Mavara.

But the young count had managed to avoid trouble and Andrei hoped he would be able to soothe Sophia enough to allow for a pleasant few days here on the estate, followed by a carefree journey for all five of them back to St Petersburg.

'Not for me, thank you,' said Valerie, as Pyotr gave orders to Feodor before escorting Sophia from the room. 'Like the countess, I feel in need of sleep and will see you in the morning.'

She knew Tassya's young heart had been awakened by the gentle fair-haired officer, and hoped that they would enjoy the rest of that evening together.

⋆ ⋆ ⋆

The following days passed swiftly but Valerie was never able to see Tassya alone and speak to her about Father Grigorii. On the last morning at Mavara, Tassya placed a little packet on the breakfast table.

'That is for you, Valerie,' she said. 'As I am so excited about our train journey and won't be able to think sensibly from now on, I want you to have this at once.'

Carefully Valerie unwrapped the present and found a delicate white lace handkerchief inside.

'Oh, Tassya, thank you. It is the prettiest one I have ever owned.'

Tassya beamed. 'I knew you would like it. You can give me my present when we have finished eating, Valerie.'

Then she wanted to know if she would be allowed to come across to Alexander Palace and meet Grand Duchess Olga, of whom she had heard so much.

'I have suggested that Tassya comes over to visit us in Tsarskoe Selo and sees our apartment,' said Andrei, who had just come in. 'Then she will see the Imperial park. But you will have to make arrangements with the family, Valerie, if a meeting with the grand duchess can be agreed.'

Valerie nodded, her thoughts racing. It was not the meeting with Grand Duchess Olga that would be difficult. She was sure that could easily be arranged. It was the meeting with Grigorii Rasputin that was the problem.

Anna Vyrubova's house could be used again and would make the perfect setting for Tassya's introduction to the holy man. But how could Valerie prevent Pyotr from knowing about his sister's meeting with the man he detested?

8

Tsarskoe Selo

'Of course Tassya Silakov may come to visit us,' said Grand Duchess Olga, when Valerie returned to Alexander Palace and told her what she planned. 'I shall ask Anna Vyrubova to come upstairs when she leaves Mama, and you can explain to her.

'But we must act quickly, Valerie. Soon we will travel down to the Crimea and Father Grigorii will be returning to his village for the summer months.'

The journey back to St Petersburg had gone without a hitch. And at the huge Nicholas Station, Sophia had been met by a smartly uniformed coachman. They had all watched outside in the yard as he had lifted Tassya's chair up into the Lukaev's spacious carriage. There was room enough for Tassya, and Sophia, and all their luggage, but the two maids, Dunya and Vera, had to sit in front with the coachman.

After waving them farewell, Valerie and Dashka with the two officers had taken a drozhky to Tsarskoselsky Station, where they had caught a train the short distance to Tsarskoe Selo.

Throughout the entire journey Pyotr had ignored Valerie.

He had tried to enter her room that night at Mavara but, on finding his entrance barred despite his whispered pleas, he had had to return to his own chamber furious and disappointed.

So he had concentrated on Sophia and his sister during the journey north, hoping that Valerie would be upset by his lack of interest and regret what he regarded as her immature and foolish behaviour.

But Valerie had other things on her mind.

Once back with her beloved family, both Olga and Tatiana had been intrigued by the thought of meeting Tassya, and of helping her through their Friend.

The younger ones were still at their lessons when Anna Vyrubovu came bustling up to the girls' private sitting room and quickly agreed to contacting Father Grigorii.

'I must ask permission from the Empress,' she said, 'and do not forget that Father Grigorii is a very busy man. But if they both agree to this meeting, and if we can find a convenient day, it will be a pleasure to welcome little Tassya to my home.'

'Dear Anna.' Olga rose and walked over to

kiss the woman's soft white cheek. 'You are so good to us. No wonder Mama says she cannot manage without you.'

Anna blushed, folding plump hands across her stomach, and gazing at the grand duchess with the devoted eyes of a spaniel.

'You are my family,' she said, 'and I shall always do anything I can to help you.'

She glanced at Valerie with a sweet smile.

'Perhaps you can send a message to Tassya and tell her the day she should come here, once I have given it to you? But send someone trustworthy, Valerie. Messages and letters can be dangerous.'

She explained that the year before some letters from the Empress to Rasputin had been stolen, then given to the newspapers.

'And because the Empress loves him as we *all* do, her words were misconstrued. Soon the whole of St Petersburg was whispering about the love affair between Empress Alexandra and the man from Siberia.' She shuddered, her full cheeks wobbling in dismay.

'It was most distressing for all of us,' said Olga, 'and Papa was very angry. But Mama remained calm, as she always does, and eventually all the horrid gossip died down.'

No wonder Sophia said such unpleasant things about Father Grigorii, thought Valerie. Rumour and gossip would always spread about important people and the more they spread, the more the rumours would be embroidered.

'That is why Our Friend uses my house for our meetings and seldom comes to the palace,' said Anna.

'Unless Alexis needs him,' said Tatiana softly.

Anna nodded. 'When the tsarevich is bleeding there is only one person who can heal him.'

'I will send Dashka,' said Valerie. 'As soon as you know which days are acceptable let me know.'

★   ★   ★

The final stroke of good fortune was to hear that Pyotr and Andrei would be away for three weeks on manoevres with their regiment at Krasnoe Selo.

'Mama says you may take the carriage to meet little Tassya at the railway station,' said Olga, who had brought the news about Pyotr's absence. 'And she can spend the night here at the palace as her brother is away.' She handed Valerie a slip of paper. 'These are the days Our Friend can come and take tea at Anna's.'

It was just as well she hadn't mentioned

Grigorii Rasputin's name to Tassya at Mavara, thought Valerie, as she went to write her note. And she didn't intend mentioning the healer's name now.

Tassya was excited enough about coming to St Petersburg and the thought of meeting the Imperial family in their own home would only excite her further.

Valerie was going to invite Tassya to Alexander Palace for two days and announce that it was by command of the Empress. That would make Tassya hug herself with joy.

Then Father Grigorii and his amazing healing powers could be explained once she was safely there.

★   ★   ★

The visit of Tassya Silakov to Alexander Palace was a great success. The grand duchesses were enchanted with Pyotr's pretty sister, and she was overwhelmed by all the grandeur.

'It's like the Lukaev's mansion,' she told Valerie, 'only *much* finer! But the grand duchesses are so simple and unaffected they are like us.'

That afternoon the two girls were getting ready for the tea party at Anna's house. Tassya was sharing Valerie's bedroom where two more beds had been installed, one for her and one for Dunya.

The maid-servant had never slept on a bed before, and as she pushed her mistress's chair around, her eyes were almost popping out of her broad Slavic face.

'Is this Anna Vyrubova also easy to talk to?' said Tassya. 'And will the Imperial family be joining us for tea?'

Tassya, who was dressed in a neat brown wool dress with matching slippers, looked as curious and excited as her maid. What memories she would have to take back with her to Mavara.

'There will only be you and I at Anna's,' said Valerie. 'Although she may be expecting another visitor.'

Perhaps, if her plan worked, Tassya would be able to come north more often? If Father Grigorii could help her to walk again, the journey to St Petersburg would not be a problem, and Tassya would be able to visit her brother, and Andrei, several times a year.

Valerie wished that she could be around to watch the drama unfold. But it seemed more than likely that she would have to return to England once this year was over.

Sighing, she nodded at Dunya to wheel the chair out into the corridor where two footmen, in black velvet jackets and scarlet

137

breeches, came to carry it down the stairs.

Fortunately it wasn't snowing and, although there was still plenty carpeting the ground, the path had been shovelled free making their progress easy.

The last time Valerie had been this way she had bumped into Pyotr, who had guessed at her meeting with Rasputin. How glad she was that *this* time he was safely away from Tsarskoe Selo and unable to spoil the thrill and anticipation of the great man's visit.

Father Grigorii was sitting in the same chair by the fire when Anna escorted her guests into the front parlour. Valerie clenched her fists tightly at her sides as she watched Anna wheel Tassya forward. Dunya had been sent off to the kitchen so there were only the four of them in the small, cosily furnished room.

But the moment Tassya stared into the darkly-bearded face of the black-robed man, she was smiling.

The holy man did not rise, but gently took one of Tassya's hands in his, as her chair was wheeled up close to his. He spoke about his village in Siberia and the girl was fascinated by his tales, understanding him despite his thick accent, and never taking her eyes off his face,

After the tea things had been cleared away, he asked for Tassya to lie on the chaise longue that stood against the wall.

'I want the child to be totally calm,' he said to Anna.

Once again Valerie felt uncomfortable. She was sure Pyotr's sister would be safe with both her and Anna Vyrubova present, but she hoped Father Grigorii wouldn't pull back Tassya's skirts and allow her poor legs to be in full view. Nor did she want him to touch the girl's body.

To her relief, he did not attempt to lift Tassya from her chair, but called for Dunya and the other maid-servant to come from the kitchen.

Once she was lying flat on the chaise longue looking up at him, he stood over her one hand clasping the heavy gold cross on his chest, the other stretched out over her body some inches above her.

Slowly he began to pray, speaking so quietly that Valerie couldn't hear him and Tassya, whose eyes were closed, looked as if she was falling asleep.

Could he do anything for her? Would his amazing powers work for little Tassya Silakov? Valerie found she was holding her breath in that hushed atmosphere.

Suddenly Rasputin's voice rang out so loudly that it made both Valerie and Anna jump.

'Open your eyes and look at me, Tassya Silakov!'

Tassya's eyes flew open as the tense body of the man bent over her, speaking more quietly, but with great persuasion. He was willing her to recover.

In the lamplight Valerie saw the same sheen of perspiration on his brow and on his cheeks above his beard, which she had noticed the night he left the bedside of the tsarevich.

Then Tassya cried out, and Valerie would never forget the look of rapture on the girl's face.

'My toes,' she said, her voice hoarse with emotion, 'I can feel my toes.'

As Valerie and Anna looked down at her little brown slippers that were protruding beneath the folds of her brown wool dress, they saw slight, very slight, movement.

★ ★ ★

Back at Alexander Palace all the grand duchesses gathered in the girls' sitting room to find out how Tassya had fared with Father Grigorii. Even Alexis joined them for a while, intrigued by the girl in the wheelchair and aware for the first time of another young person who was unable to lead a normal life.

'Our Friend will make you better,' he said

confidently. 'He always helps me when I am suffering.'

Tassya nodded, her blue eyes sparkling as she looked round at so many sympathetic and interested faces.

'He has told me what movements to practise, and to go and see him again in St Petersburg.'

'But how can you visit without Sophia knowing?' cried Valerie. 'She is sure to forbid it. You know she doesn't believe in the holy man.'

Then she would tell Pyotr and he would have his sister sent back to Mavara at once.

'I have thought it all out,' said Tassya calmly, 'and will be able to do it without Sophia knowing a thing.'

'How will you do that?' asked Olga, admiring the girl who, despite her crippled state, possessed such courage and determination.

'The Lukaevs have said I may use one of their carriages whenever I wish,' said Tassya, with a grin. 'So I shall go out with Dunya on little excursions and she and the coachman won't tell tales.'

'For how long will you be staying in St Petersburg?' asked Valerie.

She trusted Father Grigorii. She could not believe the unpleasant gossip about him coming from Mrs Lees, and Sophia, and

Pyotr. But she also knew it was not correct for a man and young girl to be left alone together. And this was *her* plan and if anything went wrong it would be *her* fault.

'You are looking worried, Valerie.' Tatiana's voice broke into her thoughts. 'What is troubling you? Do you not have faith in Our Friend?'

'Indeed I do!' said Valerie, blood rushing to her cheeks as they all stared at her. 'But I was wishing we were not going so far away and could see any improvements as they occur.'

'Sophia says I can stay as long as I like,' said Tassya. 'So I will probably still be here when you get back from the Crimea and then you will see very noticeable improvements!'

★ ★ ★

When Pyotr and Andrei returned to Tsarskoe Selo with their regiments, all was hustle and bustle as the family prepared to travel south for Easter.

Two days before they departed, Dashka came to find Valerie who was sitting sewing with Olga and Tatiana, and informed her that she had a visitor.

'Count Silakov wishes to see you, bárishna,' she said, bobbing a curtsey, 'and awaits you downstairs.'

Had he found out about Tassya's meetings with Rasputin? Valerie's heart plunged to the soles of her grey slippers. Had something dreadful happened to his sister in St Petersburg?

'Go at once, Valerie,' said Olga, watching the blood drain from the English girl's face.

Valerie placed her needlework on the table beside her then stood up and smoothed down her skirts.

'I won't be long,' she said, attempting a smile, before following the maid out of the room.

Downstairs in a small antechamber leading from the main hallway, Pyotr was waiting. He was about to go off duty, but had chosen this moment to call and see his Varinka.

When he had informed Andrei of his idea, his friend had frowned.

'You will have to tread carefully with your Little England,' he had said. 'I believe she loves you despite the extraordinary ups and downs in your relationship, and will gladly spend the rest of her life with you here in Russia. But as your wife, Petya, not your mistress.'

'I shall explain to her that cannot be,' said Pyotr grimly.

It was so clear to him. The enormous problem and the obvious solution.

'For heaven's sake!' he said, wishing Andrei would show more enthusiasm for his idea. 'Having a mistress is an accepted fact these days, even the Imperial family have experienced it. The Tsar's grandfather had his Catherine for fourteen years whilst Empress Marie still lived.'

'You are being carried away by your emotions, Petya. The present Tsar and Empress are the ones Valerie loves and there is no mistress for Tsar Nicholas, as we all know. He and Alexandra are a most devoted couple and it is *their* example that your Little England will wish to follow.'

'Not when she hears me out,' said Pyotr stubbornly. 'I know my Varinka loves me and when I offer her a home, and all the servants she requires, I know she will agree.'

Andrei shrugged, unimpressed by such fervour.

'Do not forget that she has proved as obstinate as a mule in the past. And what of Sophia? How is she going to accept this?'

'Sophia will possess my title, and will be mistress of Mavara, which is what she has always wanted,' he said.

'Then I wish you well, my friend, and hope all goes as you desire it. But be prepared for some surprises, Petya. Life has a way of upsetting even the best laid plans.'

Pyotr, however, had been confident and very determined. Nothing and no-one was going to stop him achieving his dream.

But as he waited for Valerie to join him, he decided not to confront her with his plan immediately. That could wait until the warm climes of the Crimea had been reached. All he wanted at present was to see her and talk to her, and bring their stormy relationship back onto an even keel.

And the moment Valerie caught sight of him, her heart rose as if on wings, beating against her ribs like a wild bird desperate to break free from its cage. Pyotr didn't look angry and was smiling with such genuine pleasure she had difficulty in not running forward and flinging herself into his arms.

But she advanced slowly, then stopped sedately in front of him.

'Valerie — how I have missed you.' He reached forward to take her right hand in his. 'Absence really does make the heart grow larger.'

'Fonder,' she said.

'Fonder, yes, and it was while I was away in Krasnoe Selo that I realized how much you mean to me.'

His eyes caressed her face and his thick, dark hair fell across his brow making her long to smooth back his ruffled curls.

His overcoat lay across the back of a chair where he had flung it, and his fur hat was on the seat, leaving him standing tall and lean and splendid in his immaculate winter uniform.

Everything about Count Pyotr Silakov was magnificent, from the gold epaulettes on his shoulders down to the highly polished sheen of his black riding boots and silver spurs.

'Is that what you came to see me about?' she asked.

Pyotr nodded. It didn't matter that she was wearing her usual grey-blue attire. He had seen her in white satin and pearls at the Winter Palace, and in stunning apple-green and gold at Mavara. His Little England could dress as elegantly as any princess if circumstances demanded it.

He lifted her hand and held it against his chest.

'I also came to thank you for taking care of Tassya whilst I was away, and to tell you how much I am looking forward to our days down in the Crimea.'

She smiled up at him. He didn't know about Rasputin.

'I'm glad your sister is happy,' she said, 'and I am also looking forward to the warmth of the south.'

She loved him, she couldn't help it. And

down in the Crimea she would see more of Pyotr, and there would be no Sophia hovering in the background.

'Indeed, it will be summer when we get to the coast so take plenty of light clothing with you,' he said, longing to pull her towards him and kiss her joyful face. But there would be time enough for that in the glorious days ahead. 'You will also be experiencing your first Easter in Russia, Varinka, which will be another occasion to remember.'

He bent his dark head and touched her fingers with his lips.

'I do not expect we will see each other on the journey, so enjoy your travel with the family but think of *me*, Varinka. I shall be waiting for you in Livadia.' He released her hand and bowed, before striding to the door and holding it open for her. 'Farewell, my love.'

Valerie found herself smiling again, and wanting to sing and dance all the way up the stairs to the next floor. Despite Sophia and her wealth, and despite Tassya's belief that her brother had to wed the Petersburg beauty, Valerie felt hope rising in her breast.

Miracles did happen. And if her faith was strong enough she would marry Pyotr, and Tassya would walk again.

9

The Crimea – Easter 1914

The Imperial train was a travelling palace and the best possible way of crossing the wide expanse of Russia. There were rooms for the grand duchesses and for Alexis, as well as a separate coach for the Tsar and Empress, and they were all painted white inside and royal blue outside, with the double-eagled crest in gold decorating the sides of the compartments.

When the Imperial family and their servants, accompanied by various court officials, all boarded the train in St Petersburg, Valerie was surprised to see two identical trains standing side by side.

'Why two?' she asked Olga, as they hurried along the platform with both engines puffing in readiness to depart, and strings of blue carriages emblazoned with the gold crest waiting behind them.

The girls were carrying light bags with books and shawls for their long journey south.

'There are always two trains that travel a few miles apart so nobody can be sure which one we are in,' said Olga. Glancing at her companion's face she slowed down, putting out her free hand to pat Valerie's arm.

'Do not worry, dear friend, we have not been blown up so far, and I cannot believe anything bad will happen whilst you are with us.'

The entire Tsarskoselsky Station was surrounded by armed guards and police, and no other train would be allowed to arrive or depart until the two for the Imperial family had left St Petersburg.

'Come along, this is the one for us, in you get and I'll show you our apartments.'

Trying to forget what Olga had just told her, Valerie climbed into the carriage and gazed around her.

The sitting room for the Empress was furnished in her favourite mauve and white, the Tsar's private study was all green leather and dark brown wood, and the dining compartment held kitchen equipment, wine cabinets, and a long table, which could easily sit twenty people.

'This is ours,' said Olga, enjoying her friend's amazement as she led her into a pretty chintz room, where pink roses and green leaves decorated the chair covers and curtains. Everything was so normal with bookshelves, and a table, and another door opening into a bedroom, Valerie couldn't believe she was standing in a railway train.

Grand Duchess Olga, to whom all this was commonplace, smiled happily.

'Mama and Papa have a special bath that is so cleverly designed that water won't fall out even if we are travelling round a bend!' she said. 'But I'm afraid we have to make do with a basin until we reach Livadia.'

'I don't mind,' said Valerie, thinking that a basin would not be too difficult with so many luxuries all about her.

*   *   *

Her first impression of Livadia Palace, built high on the cliffs overlooking the Black Sea, was of warmth. Gone were the frosts and snows that had surrounded Alexander Palace, and here she gloried in the flowering shrubs and blossoms that encircled the sun-kissed residence. It was summer, at last.

'I knew you would like it here,' said Olga, on the first day, taking her arm and propelling her along the corridor then down the stairs to a wide marbled hall and out into the courtyard beyond. 'This new palace was completed three years ago and we are thrilled with it. Come and see the gardens, and the wonderful view of the sea.'

'Why is it a new palace?' asked Valerie, almost running to keep up with her companion. 'What was here before?'

'A dreadful old place, ancient and gloomy, all made of wood,' said Olga.

The gardens were laid out with large triangular flowerbeds amidst the various lawns, and the scent of lilacs and roses filled the balmy air. Behind the palace were tall cypress trees and beyond them orchards and vineyards rose to the hills, protecting the small peninsular from cold north winds.

'It was worth the journey, wasn't it?' said Olga, gathering up her white skirts and dancing ahead of Valerie over the emerald turf.

It certainly was, thought Valerie.

All the girls had changed into white dresses for their stay in such a warm climate, as had the Empress and Anna Vyrubova, and the sight of their large straw hats decorated with flowers, lace-trimmed parasols, long white gloves and white silk stockings, filled Valerie with more pleasure.

She had had some dresses made for her of cotton and muslin, which were deliciously light and cool to wear and made her feel very feminine and attractive. She hoped Pyotr would be impressed by her new look when he next saw her.

'Mama likes us to go around the various sanatoria at least once a week,' Olga told Valerie on their second day. 'You may come with us, if you'd like.'

'I would love to,' said Valerie. 'I can see by your face that it's one of your favourite duties.'

'I love it! Tatiana is not so keen and Anna does her best when she accompanies Mama, but she finds it very wearisome.'

The following afternoon, early after lunch, the carriage was waiting for them and the three girls set off with Count Pyotr Silakov in attendance.

'Mama and Papa do not like us travelling alone even in this peaceful part of the world,' said Olga, smiling across at Pyotr. She was sitting beside her sister in the open carriage and Valerie and the young officer faced them.

It was the first time Valerie had seen Pyotr since leaving Tsarskoe Selo, and she noticed how the strong southern sunshine had already darkened his skin, making his eyes a more vivid blue and his teeth appear even whiter.

'How are you enjoying the Crimea, Miss Marsh?' he asked formally, as the carriage began its slow progress up into the hills.

'Very much, thank you,' said Valerie, feeling her own cheeks darken and wishing he was not sitting quite so close to her.

'For someone who has been in Russia for such a short time, you have seen many parts of our great land,' said Pyotr, thinking how fresh and pretty she looked in her white lace, edged with pink ribbon. His Little England was like strawberries and cream — good enough to eat. 'You have seen St Petersburg and the frozen north, been down to Mavara in the Ukraine, and are now in the Crimea. Whatever next, I wonder?'

'The Standart next,' said Olga. 'Our beautiful yacht, which will take us along the fjords of Finland and then on to the hunting lodges of Poland for the autumn.'

Valerie was shaking her head, making the rosebuds on the brim of her straw hat bobble and dance.

'I cannot believe all this is happening to me!' she cried. 'I keep thinking I'll wake up in Putney and find I've been dreaming.'

'It is not a dream,' said Tatiana firmly. 'This is truly you, Valerie Marsh, riding in a carriage with two grand duchesses and a count, not forgetting the coachman,' she added quickly, making them all laugh.

The rest of that afternoon was spent in sombre mood with Valerie and Pyotr walking behind the grand duchesses as they made a tour of a sanatorium.

Although their backs were aching, their feet burning, their heads spinning, from hours of standing and walking and talking, the two sisters remained as interested during the final farewells as they had been when entering the institution.

It was only when they were back in the carriage and making a faster downhill trot homewards, that Olga leaned back in her seat and closed her eyes, knocking her hat askew.

'My feet!' she whimpered, kicking off her smudged white shoes and crinkling up her toes in her now grey stockings.

'It's my back!' yelped Tatiana, who was tall like her mother, and some inches bigger than her sister.

'Everything aches in my body,' said Valerie, 'and *I* didn't have to talk and ask intelligent questions.' She smiled across at her two tired companions.

Olga nodded. 'We'll visit another place soon,' she said.

'But not tomorrow!' cried Tatiana and Valerie at the same time.

As Pyotr watched the weary, contented faces opposite him, he wished everyone in Russia could know the Imperial family as he did, then he glanced down at Valerie's tired face and wanted to smile. He was sure 1914 was going to be the start of a good life for them. He would tell her his plans as soon as he could get her on her own.

★ ★ ★

Easter, as Pyotr had informed Valerie, was another occasion she would never forget. Although she was a parson's daughter and had always thought her father a deeply religious man, he was not as devout as Empress Alexandra.

They arrived in the Crimea on the Saturday before Palm Sunday, and the Empress attended services in the chapel twice a day in Holy Week.

'We don't go quite so often,' Olga told Valerie, 'and you needn't come with us as you are not of the Orthodox Russian faith. But please come on Holy Thursday, as that is a very special day for us.'

Happily Valerie agreed to accompany them and, although she couldn't understand what was being said during the service, she loved the musical sound of the Russian language in her ears, and the smell of incense in her nostrils.

From every corner of the church golden icons glittered in the candle-light and from the iconostasis, the high screen before the altar, diamonds and emeralds and rubies

155

blazed out their fabulous wealth. Yet peasant women wearing simple cotton headscarves were standing next to court officials and their wives, and Valerie felt very content in the atmosphere of such deep faith, and the drawing together of people from such different walks of life.

On Easter Eve there was a procession with candles all through the courts of Livadia Palace led by the priest, Father Agathon, who looked remarkably like Grigorii Rasputin. He wore his black hair long on his shoulders and also possessed a full black beard.

But there were no black robes nor long black boots for Father Agathon. Instead, he wore a magnificent coat embroidered with silver and gold, and was almost enveloped in a cloud of blue smoke from the swaying censer in his hand.

To Valerie's surprise, and joy, Pyotr slipped into step beside her carrying a candle in his right hand.

'Wait and see what happens when we reach the church, Varinka,' he said.

Olga and her family were right up at the front of the procession so Valerie, following some distance behind them and surrounded by strangers, was delighted to have Pyotr beside her.

Like a river of light the mass of people

wound its way between marble columns and across tiled courtyards, until it reached the door of the chapel. Father Agathon looked inside and, finding it empty, turned to face the crowd of expectant people behind him. With a great cry of triumph he shouted into the warm night air.

'Khristos Voskrese!'

Tears stung Valerie's eyes at the sound of exultation in his voice, and excitement rose in her heart. She knew what those words meant. Christ is risen!

Then a huge roar went up all around her as the people replied.

'Voistinu Voskrese!'

Through her tears, Valerie muttered — 'He is risen indeed.'

Easter had never been like this during her father's austere, rather stern services. Was it because her own people lacked the vibrant, passionate, almost gypsy-like character of the Russian folk? There was warmth in their voices and in their enraptured faces, which awakened strong emotions within her own breast and, looking up at Pyotr so tall and immensely virile beside her, she desired him more than ever before.

As if feeling her burning gaze, Pyotr glanced down and then placed an arm around her shoulders and gave her a tight bear's hug.

'Oh, my Varinka, was that not wonderful? Was it not a very special occasion?' He held her close as the crowds milled around, his lips against her hair.

'It was the most moving church ceremony I have ever witnessed,' she said, pressing her face against his light shirt and feeling the heat of his body, and the thudding of his heart, through the white cotton.

'This is my Russia, Varinka,' he said fiercely. 'The land I will gladly give my life for!'

'Don't say that!' Valerie drew away from his embrace and frowned up at him. 'Don't ever speak of death, Pyotr Silakov. You must only think of life.'

Her eyes flashed as she clutched at his sleeve, wanting to shake him out of such morbid patriotism.

'Life *and* love, Little England?' At once he was smiling, amused by her anger and delighted by her concern.

'Life and love,' she agreed, leaning against his powerful body once more. This was the Crimea, this was summer, and she would worry about morals and good behaviour once she returned to the icy north.

'You must go in now,' he said, as they walked slowly hand-in-hand back towards the palace apartments, 'and I must return to my duties. But I will see you tomorrow, Varinka, to wish you a happy Easter Day.'

Pyotr pulled her round to face him. He bent forward and touched her forehead with his lips, then the tip of her small nose, before lowering his head and covering her mouth with his.

It was the first time he had kissed her since that night at Mavara, so long ago it seemed now, and as the parched earth absorbs the summer rain Valerie opened her lips, and her arms, to receive his searching, demanding love.

10

On Easter Day, Livadia Palace became one great banqueting hall.

Because the Lenten fast was over, everyone was able to eat what they wanted and tables were laid out through the downstairs rooms with food and wine available all that day and night.

There were roasted suckling pigs, lambs, and chickens, geese with apples and many sorts of fish with salted cucumbers. The traditional dessert of rich and creamy paskha was there, as well as Easter cakes covered in white icing and decorated with a cross.

Later, servants passed around trays of chocolates, caramels, nuts, figs, dates and crystallized fruits.

Valerie had never seen such an array of food, and the tables seemed to sag beneath so much fare as hundreds of guests arrived to take part in the joyous celebrations.

It was an exhausting time for Tsar Nicholas and Empress Alexandra for they presided over all the comings and goings, greeting every member of their household with kisses and presents.

The Empress looked beautiful, but very tired in her long dress of white chiffon, edged with lace.

'It is so nice to have you with us, Valerie,' she said, leaning forward to kiss the girl twice on one cheek and once on the other. 'These are our traditional kisses of blessing, welcome, and joy, my dear. And here is a small gift for you on this happiest of occasions.'

Anna Vyrubova stood immediately behind the Empress, handing her little packages, which were laid out on the table beside her. She gave Alexandra one such package, which the Empress then placed in Valerie's hands.

'I hope it will please you, dear Valerie, and always remind you of your stay in this glorious land of ours.'

When Valerie moved away allowing other members of the household and of the court, and of the Imperial Guard, to step forward in their turn, she opened the small box to find a perfect jewelled flower nestling inside.

Its leaves were of green enamel and mother-of-pearl, with petals of pink enamel, and the stem was of gold with the centre of tiny diamonds bedded in more gold.

She stared at the exquisite piece in silence. It was the most beautiful — certainly the most expensive — object she had ever owned.

'What have you got?' Suddenly Olga

appeared beside her, peering down at her gift. 'Oh, I'm so glad it's that one! I told Mama you would like it, but she always has to make her own choice.'

'It is quite perfect,' said Valerie huskily.

'Now, now, Valerie, you are getting emotional and that will not do!' said the grand duchess, putting her arm around the English girl's shoulders. Then she caught sight of Pyotr advancing towards them, and sighed with relief. 'Come and distract our Little England's attention, Count Silakov. She is going to weep all over her Easter present from Mama!'

Pyotr halted in front of the girls then leaned down to place a kiss on Valerie's pink cheek.

'Was that for blessing, welcome, or joy?' asked Olga.

'For joy,' he said, smiling. 'And I also have a present for our English visitor, but it will be insignificant when compared to the Fabergé she now holds in her hands.' His mouth twisted in a mournful grimace. 'I am ashamed to offer this, Miss Marsh, but it is to wish you a happy first Easter in Russia.'

Once again Valerie fought to control her emotion. It was all too much this generosity, especially when she had nothing to give in return. But her face glowed at the sound of

Pyotr's deep voice and she held out her right hand for his gift, thanking him with her eyes.

'I have nothing for you,' she said, 'because I did not know Easter was such an important celebration here, but I am deeply grateful for your kindness.'

As she took his package their fingers touched for one fleeting moment.

'Open it!' said Olga, removing the Fabergé from Valerie's left hand and leaning forward to see what else her friend had received. 'I have a feeling your present will be far more valuable to her than Mama's,' she told the young officer.

Pyotr grinned, but said nothing as he watched Valerie open his gift.

It was a simple egg, which had been hard-boiled then painted with the finest of brush-strokes forming minute pictures of flowers, and birds, and butterflies. The colours were brilliant and as Valerie held it on the palm of her hand, she revelled in such artistry.

'Thank you with all my heart,' she said, looking up at him with the joy he loved to see. 'I shall treasure it always.'

She placed the egg carefully back in its box and closed the lid.

'I wish you would be less formal with each other,' said Olga impetuously, 'and say what you really mean. I know you think of each other as Valerie and Pyotr, so why not say so? But you,' she said to Pyotr, 'keep calling her Miss Marsh, and Valerie doesn't call you anything at all!'

'Olga Nicolaievna, you are a great adviser,' he said gruffly, 'but you should not encourage me in my amorous intentions towards the little foreigner.'

The grand duchess laughed.

'You would not harm our Little England, dear count, for you love her as sincerely as we do. Now, Valerie, control your blushes and come with me before the handsome count decides to kiss you again. There is a ball here tomorrow night and we must go and decide on what to wear. I hope you will be attending, Count Silakov?'

'I shall certainly be attending, Olga Nicolaievna, and hope that you will honour me with a dance?'

'I will gladly dance with you, if Valerie will allow it?'

'Whatever Your Imperial Highness commands,' said Valerie, falling into a deep curtsey.

Olga smiled and hauled her to her feet.

'Come on, we'll go and see how to make ourselves beautiful for the evening!'

★   ★   ★

It was a magical evening that night of the ball in the state ballroom of Livadia Palace.

Tatiana and Olga wore filmy white gowns decorated with lace, and clusters of pink roses adorned their breasts and waists.

Valerie was in rose-pink chiffon with deeper red roses at her waist and breast.

All three girls had piled their hair high with diamond pins embedded in their shining curls, and Valerie felt as grand as she had felt at the ball in the Winter Palace in St Petersburg. She longed to see Pyotr and surprise him all over again.

When they went downstairs, the glass doors at the far end of the ballroom had been opened onto the garden, and Valerie could hear music from an unseen orchestra floating towards her on the warm sea air.

In the ballroom lights from the chandeliers sparkled onto the hundreds of guests. All the women wore soft floating gowns, many glittering with diamonds, and the men wore crisp white uniforms decorated with gold braid and various medals.

The younger children were not present, but Valerie saw the Tsar and Empress sitting at a table near the entrance, and she thought how relaxed and happy they looked. Empress Alexandra did not dance, but Tsar Nicholas moved sedately around the floor with several different ladies, and when he had Olga or Tatiana in his arms, the pride on his fine bearded face was a pleasure to behold.

'You are happy, Varinka?' said Pyotr, who had come to claim her.

'I have never been so happy,' she said, as they danced in unison to the lilting refrains of a waltz. 'I wish I could stay for longer in this beautiful land. It is like a fairy tale come true for me.'

Looking down at her in his arms, thinking she looked lovelier than he had ever seen her, Pyotr decided to wait no longer.

'Would you stay in Russia with me, if I asked it of you, Varinka?'

'Remain here — always?' She stared up at him, her heart pounding beneath her tight bodice. 'You want me to stay with you, Pyotr?'

He nodded, drawing her to one side, out of the way of the other dancers.

'We do not know each other very well,' he said, finding the words harder than he had anticipated. 'And it will mean leaving your country, and your father. You will make a new life far away from your family and friends. Would you do that for me?'

He had to make sure she knew exactly what she was doing. This was no fleeting, superficial affair like the many he had had in the past. This was total commitment. Till eternity. *He* was quite certain how he felt, but he had to be sure his Little England felt that way too.

'I will gladly stay with you forever, Pyotr Silakov,' said Valerie, with a decided nod of her diamond-decked head.

'Then let us go through those doors away from all this noise,' he said, 'and all these people.'

He placed one of her small gloved hands on his arm, then led her out into the garden. They walked past other sauntering couples up a narrow, gently winding path until they were alone in the moonlight.

Standing together high on the cliffs overlooking the silvery waters of the Black Sea, Pyotr turned Valerie round to face him.

'You know I love you, Varinka, and intend loving you for the rest of my life,' he said, his eyes black in the semi-darkness.

She gave a deep sigh. 'I know. And I love you very much and will endeavour to make you a good wife, Pyotr.'

My God! She didn't understand. Why did his plan seem so easy in his mind yet so devilishly awkward to explain?

He clutched her shoulders. 'Valerie, listen to me. We cannot marry, my darling. I thought you realized that. I *must* marry Sophia.'

Her body went rigid under his hands as she

tried to pull away.

'You said you loved me: You said you wanted to live with me forever!'

'I *do*! I have worked it all out most thoughtfully and wonderfully. It is truly a good idea, Varinka, and will allow us the love we both desire so much.'

Pyotr held her tighter, not allowing her to break away.

'I will look after you for eternity — promise you that.'

His voice deepened, thick with passion. He *had* to make her understand.

'I want you so much, my heart, and will love and cherish you forever. Say yes, Varinka, say you will come with me and be my love.'

'You mean be your mistress.' Valerie's throat was so constricted she could scarcely speak. 'You mean that, don't you, Pyotr?'

What would she tell Olga? How could she explain to the Empress? And how could she write to her father and tell him and Mrs Duffy that she would be remaining in Russia as the kept woman of an impoverished nobleman?

★   ★   ★

Of course she should have known that it was not possible to marry Pyotr — but she had

168

hoped. She loved him very much, but she wanted to be his wife. She was not going to be tucked away somewhere and visited when he could spare the time.

As Pyotr's hands fell from her shoulders, Valerie turned and walked away from him. She didn't hurry, but moved with a straight back, her head held high, as her heart splintered into a thousand pieces.

11

St Petersburg

Although Olga and Tatiana had been longing to hear how her love affair with Count Pyotr Silakov was progressing, Valerie told them nothing. How could she explain that he wanted to share her with another woman?

'Please exclude me from any duties in future when the count is to be in attendance,' she said. 'And don't question me about him. Our friendship has ended.'

Then she hurried from the room before bursting into tears.

'Do you suppose he tried to seduce her?' asked Tatiana.

Olga frowned. 'She loved him — I know she did. And I am sure he loves her. Something bad must have happened to part them.'

'A voyage on the Standart will do her good,' said Tatiana philosophically.

'Perhaps.' Her sister was not convinced.

A letter from St Petersburg arrived the following day, giving Valerie unexpected pleasure and taking her thoughts away from her own misery.

Tassya wrote that she was feeling much better and was managing to visit Father Grigorii without being detected. She was longing to see Valerie again as she had a surprise for her.

' ... I do not know when the Imperial family intend returning to Tsarskoe Selo,' she went on, 'but I hope it will be soon, dear friend. Unhappily news from home is not good as Mother has been taken ill and wants me back. Write quickly, Valerie, and let me know when you will be here again. Your ever loving, Tassya.'

When Valerie told Olga about the letter, the grand duchess smiled.

'We go north on Friday,' she said.

★   ★   ★

A further letter awaited Valerie at Alexander Palace. Here, winter had only just departed, allowing spring flowers to lift their heads in proud splendour across the Imperial Park.

' ... Come on Thursday,' wrote Tassya, 'as the Lukaevs have been invited out for the day and I shall plead a headache and wait in the house for you. Please try and come — there is so much to tell you ... '

As she waited in the drawing room of the Lukaev's mansion, Valerie had time to feel the thick springiness of the white carpet beneath her feet and to study the many oil paintings on the walls — most of which were beautiful portraits of Sophia.

Masses of flowers were arranged in huge crystal vases standing on antique furniture and, at the far end of the spacious room, glass doors led onto a terrace.

Beside the glass doors was a grand piano and Valerie remembered that evening at Mavara when Sophia had played so well. Then Tassya entered the room behind her and all thought of Sophia vanished.

'There! I've caught you by surprise!' Tassya held out her hands as she was wheeled forward. 'Oh, Valerie, I have been waiting ages to see you — but now you are here and we have time to ourselves.'

'You are looking very well,' said Valerie, bending forward to embrace her companion.

Tassya was dressed in scarlet, a shade that suited her dark hair, and there was colour in her normally pale face and a sparkle in her blue eyes.

Dunya, standing behind the chair, was also looking plumper than Valerie remembered her.

'We shall have tea now,' said Tassya. 'Please tell Kotchka we are ready, Dunya.'

With a nod the maid-servant departed, leaving the two girls alone.

'I am feeling wonderful,' Tassya went on, 'but cannot say the same about you. Why are you so peaky and thin when you have just returned from the south? You are not sickening for something, I hope?'

'I am not ill, just a little tired. But tell me about yourself Tassya. And Father Grigorii. How is he?'

'Father Grigorii is well,' said Tassya demurely, 'and I shall only have one more meeting with him before he returns to his village in Siberia and I, alas, have to return to Mavara.'

'But it is your home, Tassya, and you must be worried about your mother. What is wrong with her?'

'Her heart is not good.' Tassya's mouth turned down at the corners. 'The doctor says she must rest so I must return to help her, but I am fearful, Valerie. Mother was difficult to please when she was well and busy, but she will make a terrible invalid. Of course I cannot do anything physically, but she wants me to sit with her, and read to her, and write all her letters for her.'

'You'll have to do your best,' said Valerie, trying to sound cheerful, 'and allow wonderful memories of St Petersburg to sustain you. Perhaps, next year, you'll be able to come north again?'

Tassya nodded, but said nothing more as Dunya returned, followed by a footman wheeling a tea-trolley laden with freshly baked brioches, a large plum cake, and a bowl of sugared hazel-nuts. Another man-servant carried in the samovar and placed it on the table beside Tassya's chair, and a third brought in a tray of crockery.

'What is your surprise, Tassya?' asked Valerie, once the footmen had departed.

'Later,' said Tassya, filling the cups with tea and passing one to her friend.

Valerie sighed, knowing she couldn't hurry Tassya. But once they had eaten all they could of the delicious food, she could hide her impatience no longer.

'Come on, *tell* me,' she said.

Tassya, with a strange expression on her face, nodded and then called over her shoulder to Dunya. The maid-servant immediately moved forward to stand beside the wheelchair. To Valerie's astonishment, Tassya then rested one hand on the maid's arm and her other on the wooden arm-rest of her chair. Then slowly and awkwardly she slid her feet forward and lowered them onto the carpet.

'Now!' she shouted.

Dunya raised the arm supporting her young mistress and Tassya released her hold on the armrest, then *stood* on the white carpet one hand still clinging to Dunya's rigid arm.

'There, Valerie Marsh!' she said, her face red with exertion. 'I am standing on my poor useless legs. Can you see me?'

'Tassya!' Valerie was clapping her hands, her eyes popping with excitement. 'It's a miracle!'

'And I can walk.' Tassya bit at her lower lip and stared straight ahead of her. 'Come on, Dunya, one, two, three!' With enormous concentration she shuffled one foot, then the other, over the carpet with the maid keeping pace beside her. 'Enough — I can't do any more.'

Quickly Dunya stretched out for the chair and placed it behind Tassya before gently pushing her mistress back onto it.

'That's better.' Tassya watched as Dunya bent and lifted her feet onto the footrest. Then she looked at Valerie. 'How about that then, Valerie Marsh?'

'It was Father Grigorii, wasn't it?' said Valerie, happiness at last brightening her face. 'He has brought life back to your legs just as he helps Alexis when he is sick.'

Tassya nodded. 'He says it will be many months before I can walk properly, but he is going to pray for me, and Dunya is to help me with my exercises.' She sighed. 'It's awfully hard making my feet move when I am tired, Valerie. But Father Grigorii says I must never give up.'

'But what does Sophia say?' said Valerie. 'What does she think has happened to you? Have you told Pyotr? What does *he* say?'

How would he react on hearing that the man he loathed was helping his sister to recover?

'Nobody knows but you and me, Valerie, and they are *not* to know. This is to be our secret until I can walk again. I am going to practise hard then invite everyone down to Mavara for my birthday. I shall have a surprise party for my friends and family!'

Valerie smiled. 'I am so pleased for you,' she said. 'And of course I'll keep your secret. But don't forget to tell everyone that it was thanks to Father Grigorii that you recovered. He is disliked by so many people this will *prove* he is a great healer and a true man of God.'

'I shall tell everyone it was Father Grigorii, and you can tell them, too, Valerie. I want you to come down to Mavara and join in my birthday celebrations.'

To return to Mavara was the last thing Valerie wanted.

'When is your birthday?' she said slowly.

'I'm not sure if I will be able to visit the Ukraine.'

'My birthday's on the first day of August and you must come, Valerie. I am sure the Imperial family will allow it when you tell them the reason, and give plenty of warning. I don't mind their knowing our secret. Ask as soon as you get back, Valerie. Promise.'

There was a fleeting glimpse of Countess Irina on Tassya's determined little face.

'I will ask, but I cannot promise to come, Tassya.'

Valerie went across to give the girl's narrow shoulders a hug. She must never allow her own bitterness and unhappiness to stand in the way of Tassya's enormous achievement.

'When does Father Grigorii leave for Siberia?' she asked, as she prepared to make her return journey to Tsarskoe Selo. 'I'd like to see him before he goes and thank him for what he has done for you.'

Tassya beamed as she gave Valerie the holy man's address in the capital.

'Then he travels east, I travel south, and you go west,' she said. 'What a busy time we'll all be having. But don't forget the first of August, Valerie,' she repeated, as Dunya wheeled her out into the hall and she waved farewell to her friend. 'Don't forget my birthday surprise!'

Sophia Lukaev sat before her mirror, taking the pearl drops from her ears, but not seeing the beautiful face that looked back at her. At last she had heard something that was very important to her. It would be the means of getting rid of that irritating foreign girl.

Vera, her maid-servant, had heard Valerie Marsh and Tassya talking that afternoon, and had informed her mistress that the English girl intended visiting Grigorii Rasputin during the coming week.

This knowledge would annoy Pyotr.

Of course it was incomprehensible that he should be interested in the penniless foreigner, and after that last evening at Mavara, Sophia was sure he only had eyes for her. But Valerie Marsh lived too close for comfort, and she had spent the last weeks with him and the Imperial family down in the warmth of the Crimea.

Sophia would not feel really confident until Pyotr's ring was on her finger and the girl had returned to England.

★ ★ ★

The following Tuesday Valerie travelled once again to St Petersburg. But this time she

178

hired a drozhky from the station that took her to the holy man's apartment. She felt guilty about taking another day away from the palace, but when she had explained to Olga, the grand duchess had smiled in delight.

'Of course you must go and thank Father Grigorii for spending some of his precious time with little Tassya,' she said. 'Mama will understand perfectly when I tell her.' Then she sighed. 'We are all so envious of you, Valerie, being able to move around unattended and now going to see Our Friend in his own home. How we would love to do that!'

Life was strange, Valerie thought, sitting on the hard flat leather cushions of the drozhky, an open carriage drawn by one horse, which was rattling its way over the cobbled streets on its iron wheels. The Imperial family possessed everything that money could buy, yet Olga longed for anonymity and freedom. And *she* would have given anything for the Lukaevs' wealth, because then she could have married the man she loved.

She had decided to come to St Petersburg without Dashka. Another rule being broken but Valerie did not care.

She should not be travelling alone. She should not be visiting the apartment of an unmarried man. Yet Olga had not tried to stop her. In fact, she had been enthusiastic about this visit and even envious of Valerie's independence.

What was more important at this time was the knowledge that the Imperial family loved and admired Rasputin just as she did, and understood her desire to show gratitude for what he had done for little Tassya.

Grigorii Rasputin's apartment was situated in the west of the city, near Nicholas Station. A man-servant opened the door to Valerie on the third floor and showed her into a large antechamber. He told her his master was eating, but said she should go through to the dining room.

As she crossed the antechamber, Valerie was surprised by the sound of voices and was immediately aware that she had come at the wrong time. She should have asked Tassya the best time to call. She certainly didn't want to see Father Grigorii in the company of others. And by the sound of it there were many female visitors.

Like a hen house, thought Valerie uncharitably, as the manservant ushered her through the open doorway.

Then she stood for a moment, stunned by what she saw.

Around a big table sat seven well-dressed Society ladies and at the head, facing the door, was Rasputin. But he was not the holy man she remembered from Anna Vyrubova's house. Nor was he the great healer she had seen standing at the foot of the tsarevich's bed.

This man was dipping his fingers into a bowl of fish in front of him and filling his mouth with the smelly mess. His beard was matted and filthy, he was using no napkin, and the potage was splashing onto his purple blouse and trickling down his sleeves.

Suddenly he caught sight of Valerie.

'English girl!' he roared. 'English girl come and eat with us.'

Two of the ladies moved apart and another chair was placed up at the table.

'You sit there.' Rasputin gestured to Valerie to take a seat.

'I am sorry.' She stepped backwards. 'I didn't know you had visitors. I'll come another time.'

She had to get away. Out of that apartment and away from that disgusting man and the smell of fish.

'You stay!' shouted Rasputin, and his man-servant moved swiftly to block her path.

In desperation Valerie looked back into the room, and saw a pleasant-faced young woman nodding and pointing at the chair next to her.

'Do come and join us,' she said. 'I will translate if you do not understand. The Master wants you to stay. We are all disciples gathered here, so please come and join us.'

Slowly Valerie walked to the chair, which was between the two who had made room for her. Perhaps she would be able to speak to Father Grigorii once this strange meeting was over? Perhaps he would become more acceptable once these women had departed?

Averting her gaze from the spattered linen cloth, the discarded crusts of black bread, and the numerous glasses and bottles of wine, Valerie folded her hands tightly on her lap and smiled faintly at the friendly woman beside her.

'Drink for our newcomer,' said Rasputin, placing a grubby hand around the bottle and pouring a glass of wine for Valerie.

She was not thirsty, but forced herself to sip at the liquid and think about Tassya. This man had helped the girl, Valerie had seen the result with her own eyes. And she had also seen how Alexis had recovered from his appalling attack of haemophilia.

Maybe this extraordinary and uncivilised behaviour was his way of relaxing? A way for him to rest his body and mind before being called yet again to use his miraculous powers of healing?

'Here, Nina, my hands are dirty. Lick them clean,' said Rasputin, holding out his slippery hands to the woman at his side.

To Valerie's horror, the woman leaned forward and began sucking at his fingers, one by one.

'The Master teaches us to be humble,' whispered the woman next to Valerie.

But not this way, thought Valerie. Her father preached often enough about the dangers of conceit and self-esteem, but the Reverend Marsh would *never* condone what Grigorii Rasputin was demanding of his followers.

Suddenly she thought of Pyotr and how he had warned her about the Siberian moujik, and how Mrs Lees had spoken of him with distaste, and how Sophia had called him a very fine man of the flesh, who cleansed women of their sins if they sinned with him first.

It was imperative that she got away — now — immediately. But how could she leave when the man-servant was still standing in the doorway? The wine was also having a strange effect on her and Valerie was not sure her feet would be firm beneath her if she stood up?

She turned her head to see her friendly neighbour smiling at her.

'When Father Grigorii has finished eating he will choose one of us to go with him to his Holy of Holies,' she said. 'Pray that you are the chosen one, my dear. It is an experience you will never forget.' Her face was alight with hope as she gazed at the man.

'Holy of Holies?' Valerie felt her stomach heave. She was going to be sick right across the table, adding to the mess of fish soup, black bread and spilled wine.

'His bedroom,' said the woman, with soft sobbing breath, 'where he teaches us love as *I* have never experienced it before. And I am a married woman, dear.'

With a cry Valerie stood up, jerking back her chair, but her legs would not hold her and she almost fell as she tried to make for the door.

'That one: I choose the English girl today!' Rasputin was rising and smiling across at Valerie.

The woman beside her caught hold of Valerie's arm.

'You are the fortunate one, and the pleasure awaiting you is out of this world. Oh, envy, envy!' She began weeping hysterically against Valerie's shoulder.

'Come, we will assist you,' said two others, coming up behind her and grabbing hold of Valerie's arms. They began propelling her away from the table and the weeping woman.

'I don't want to go!' Valerie rolled her head from side to side and tried to wrench free from their grasp. But her tongue was heavy in her mouth and her eyes wouldn't focus properly.

'You won't go yet, English girl, don't worry. You will have enjoyment first,' said one, opening the door in front of them.

She was half-carried into an ill-lit room where the curtains had not been drawn back from the windows, and a huge bed almost filled the space from wall to wall.

Valerie struggled as the women began to undress her, but her body was weak and they were too strong for her.

'Leave her.' Suddenly the Master's voice rang out. The women let go of Valerie and she fell back onto a rumpled heap of cushions and furs. 'Now go, and leave us in peace.'

The women departed, the door was closed, and Grigorii Rasputin advanced on Valerie's defenceless form.

12

Once the English girl had been joined by the Master in his Holy of Holies, the group of disciples made ready to leave the apartment. They were not wanted that day and all knew from previous experience that the Master liked to be left alone with his chosen one.

The man-servant helped the ladies with their coats and furs, then saw them away before returning to clear up the debris in the dining-room. But to his astonishment, the front door suddenly burst open and an officer of the Imperial Guard came striding into the room, fury flashing in his vivid blue eyes.

'Where is she?' He looked at the scene of spilled wine and broken bread, and smelt the fish, his nostrils flaring in revulsion. 'The English girl — where is she?' He confronted the horrified servant and felt murder in his heart.

The man knew that his master must never be disturbed at such times, but fear of the furious stranger overwhelmed him.

'In there,' he squeaked, nodding at the closed bedroom door and then retreating as fast as he could to the kitchen quarters.

* * *

Pyotr stormed through the dining-room, knocking over several chairs as he went, then wrenched open the door leading to Rasputin's inner sanctum.

For one long moment he stood staring — his worst fears realised. Valerie lay naked on the wide bed, her arms above her head in listless submission. Her eyes were closed and Pyotr prayed that she had fainted. Beside her, also naked, reclined Grigorii Rasputin, his chest almost as hairy as his bearded face. He lifted his head to look up at the intruder, his hand falling away from the girl's white body.

'Get out of here!' he shouted.

He struggled to a sitting position as Pyotr leapt forward, gathering up remnants of Valerie's clothing and flinging them over her inert body.

'Valerie, wake up! Get up!' He leaned over her, terrified she was drugged, or dead.

To his relief Valerie opened her eyes, then gazed in horror at a man's face so close to hers. But then she recognized him, and with a cry of joy flung her arms around his neck.

'Thank God,' she whispered, 'thank God you've come. Oh, take me away. Take me away from this place!'

Gathering her up in the fur on which she

was lying, Pyotr folded it carefully to hide her shame. Then he lifted her in his arms and looked down at the scowling Rasputin.

'The Empress will hear of this,' he said. 'Your days of fame and glory are over and I will see you banished to the frozen wastes from which you came.'

Then he strode out of the room and out of the apartment, carrying the trembling girl in his arms.

Below in the street his carriage was waiting and as soon as Pyotr appeared at the top of the steps with the burden in his arms, the coachman jumped from his seat and flung open the door.

'Tsarskoselsky Railway Station, bárin?' he said.

'No.' During the last painful minutes Pyotr had made up his mind. 'Bolshoy Prospect on Vassily Island,' he ordered, climbing in and cradling Valerie on his knees.

She was clinging to him as if she would never let him go, the remains of her clothing hidden somewhere amongst the folds of fur that enveloped her. Her face was against his broad chest and Pyotr could imagine her mortification and terror at what had occurred.

Valerie needed to dress herself respectably once more, and to have a good wash. The smell of fish clung to her tangled hair and his nostrils were further insulted by the odour of stale wine.

Anger swelled in Pyotr's breast. His once innocent, apple-fresh Varinka now stunk like an over-used prostitute making *him* feel in need of a wash and change of clothing.

But at the Lees' house in Bolshoy Prospect, Valerie would receive the care and attention she so desperately required. The couple were English, friends of the Marsh family, and although the large lady with the loud voice and monstrous hats had irritated him in the past, Pyotr thought she and her husband were the ideal people with whom to leave Valerie at present.

Tsarskoe Selo was too distant and Alexander Palace not the right place for the distraught girl. However, he intended going back the moment Valerie was safely settled. Empress Alexandra should be told the truth about her adored Friend and he, Pyotr Silakov, was going to tell Her Imperial Highness exactly what kind of a brute he really was.

The Empress had refused to listen to unsavoury gossip about the Siberian moujik in the past, but she had never had cause to distrust him before. Now, the girl who was companion to her eldest daughter, and whom the Imperial family had grown to love, had been most viciously assaulted by the drunken beast. Pyotr was going to demand his expulsion to Siberia — forever.

Valerie, warm in the comfort of the fur and firmly held in Pyotr's strong arms, was almost asleep. She had drunk too much wine, then been so frightened and repulsed by the fondling of that black-bearded beast, she had almost fainted.

But Pyotr had arrived when she most needed him, and with the warmth of his body close to hers — a clean healthy young body — and with the steady swaying of the carriage, she felt very secure and wanted to stay like that until slumber overtook her. She didn't want to think, or remember, or do anything except sleep.

Fortunately the Lees were at home and the moment Mrs Lees saw the handsome count standing in the hall with Valerie's limp, fur-covered body in his arms, she hurried forward, consternation clouding her face.

'What has happened to her? Has there been an accident? Oh, my dear child — is she alive?'

Mrs Lees peered forward, touching the girl's ruffled hair, gazing anxiously at her closed eyes. Then she caught a whiff of Valerie's wine-sodden breath.

'Dear Heavens!' She took a step back and glared at Pyotr. 'She is inebriated! What have you done to her, Count Silakov?'

'Is something the matter, dear?' Mr Lees came through from the library, taking in the strange scene in the hall with blinking, owl-like eyes. 'What is going on?'

'It is all right.' Pyotr endeavoured to calm the fraught atmosphere. 'Valerie is not hurt.' At least he prayed not. 'But I have taken her away from Grigorii Rasputin's apartment where too much wine was drunk. May she have a room here, Mrs Lees, until she regains her senses?'

He looked at the astonished lady with his most charming smile.

'I do not know where else to take her. She will be so ashamed when she recovers. You know what gossip is like in St Petersburg. So I said to myself, Mrs Lees is a family friend and also a very good woman.'

Mrs Lees mellowed beneath the smile and flattering words.

'Of course Valerie can stay with us,' she said, then turned and gave orders to the footman to have a room prepared and Katia sent upstairs immediately. 'You must tell me all about it another time,' she said. 'But now Valerie needs a bath and a good night's rest. That smell, Count Silakov, is quite dreadful!'

Her nose was quivering as her husband came forward to join them.

'Do not stare, Mr Lees! Valerie is in a sorry state and must be given instant attention. Poor child, I always *knew* that man was no good and I *told* her of his appalling reputation.' She paused, and Pyotr dreaded hearing what was in her mind. 'You don't suppose he — '

'You are a wonderful and understanding lady,' he said quickly, 'and I am thankful to have brought Valerie to you, Mrs Lees. Now I will carry her upstairs if you will tell me where to go, then I must leave you. I have some important business to attend to.'

'Of course.' Pushing her dumbfounded husband out of the way, Mrs Lees climbed the stairs, her mind racing.

What was Valerie doing in the Siberian peasant's apartment? And what had he done to her? If other ladies were present she supposed nothing immoral had occurred. But she had the distinct impression that Valerie was naked beneath that nasty fur. Had there been an orgy? One never knew what these foreigners would get up to next. And how had that nice count become involved? Dear me, there was so much she needed to find out in the morning.

At the top of the stairs she turned left,

leading the way across the landing to a room where the maid was hastily making up the bed.

'Hurry up, Katia,' said Mrs Lees. Then she gestured to a comfortable armchair in the corner. 'If you will put Valerie on that chair, Count Silakov, she can rest whilst a bath is run for her. Then she can go straight to bed. She looks quite exhausted, poor girl.'

Had she suffered a fate worse than death? Mrs Lees stared in horrified interest at the girl's expressionless face. Something had happened to her. She didn't look at all like the Valerie with whom she had travelled from England. Nor like the excited girl who had spent those few days at Christmas with them, and attended the Ball at the Winter Palace.

Mrs Lees didn't believe it was only too much alcohol — there was something more. And that smell. Not alcohol but fish — that was it. Valerie smelt distinctly fishy.

Settling the drowsy figure on the chair and making sure the fur still covered her inert form, Pyotr straightened and walked back to the door, leading Mrs Lees politely by the arm. If only the maid would now take charge of Valerie, she could deal with the lack of clothing and the tell-tale bruises. Pyotr did not want the Englishwoman seeing any more of the young girl's shame.

'Mrs Lees,' he said, pulling the door shut behind them, 'may I ask one more thing of you, please?'

She nodded, wondering what else was to come. Russia was a barbaric land beneath its bright extravagant surface and she was missing the solid, sensible calm of dear old England more and more.

'I would like you not to question Valerie too much in the morning,' Pyotr said carefully. 'If she wishes to speak, then it is quite in order,' he added, noticing the woman's air of disappointment.

Mrs Lees shrugged. 'Very well, I will not ask too much. But I need to know *something*, Count Silakov. What do I tell her father? And what about the Empress? Should Valerie not be returning to the palace shortly? The Imperial family will want to know what has happened to her. We must *all* be informed about what has been going on, sir.'

'I do not know myself.' He raised his hands in innocent bewilderment. 'I went only to collect Valerie Marsh and escort her back to Tsarskoe Selo, then discovered her in this sorry state. But I intend seeing Empress Alexandra at the first opportunity, and will inform her that Valerie is not well. Then I shall return for her, Mrs Lees, in a day or so and take her away from your kindness.'

Pyotr gave his disarming smile.

'Forgive me for rushing away, but I must depart.'

He bowed gracefully before hurrying down the stairs and nodding at Mr Lees, who was still pondering in the library doorway. The front door was opened by a footman and then Pyotr escaped out into the courtyard to his waiting carriage.

'Now for Tsarskoselsky Railway Station,' he told the coachman.

★   ★   ★

Fortunately, Empress Alexandra was able to see him early the following day, and when Pyotr entered her private sitting room, she was quietly at her embroidery in the company of Anna Vyrubova.

'Come in, Count Silakov,' she said, glancing up at the tall dark-haired officer and thinking, once again, how remarkably handsome he was. 'What is it you wish to see me about?'

Pyotr bowed then stood to rigid attention as he described what he had discovered the day before.

'I would beg Your Imperial Highness,' he ended, 'to have this Grigorii Rasputin sent back to where he belongs. If he remains here in the west, he will be a constant danger to the young and innocent.'

No emotion stirred on Alexandra's pale face, but her hands were still and her blue eyes became frozen.

'Father Grigorii is returning to his village at the end of this week but will come back to us in the autumn, as he always does,' she said. 'You seem to forget, Count Silakov, that Father Grigorii is Our Friend and, as such, will always have our warmest regard and affection. I fear,' she went on icily, 'that little Valerie was overcome by her devotion to the holy man and allowed her emotions full rein. She probably also partook of too much wine.'

'Forgive me, Your Imperial Highness,' said Pyotr, trying to remain courteous despite his barely concealed rage, 'but Grigorii Rasputin is known throughout St Petersburg as a lecher. And when Valerie went to ask his advice about my crippled sister, he assaulted her.'

Although confessing ignorance to Mrs Lees, Pyotr knew full well the reason for Valerie's visit.

'There are always unpleasant rumours circulating about the holy man,' said Alexandra. 'I know what people say, Count Silakov, and am not deaf to the gossip and scurrilous accusations. But folk are envious of his position at Court, and the fact that he is Our Friend, and will say anything to try to bring about his downfall.'

She turned to her companion.

'Has Father Grigorii ever attempted an immoral act, or uttered a seductive word to you, Anna?'

Anna Vyrubova shook her head, glancing from the Empress to Pyotr.

'I have often been alone with him, Your Imperial Highness,' she said, in her little girl's voice, 'and he has never been anything other than a good and pious man in my company.'

'My daughters know him and have enjoyed his friendship ever since their childhood,' went on the Empress, her voice rising, 'and we all love him as the saintly man he is. There is no question of suspecting his morals, Count Silakov.

'Now I suggest you leave the palace and take a week's leave, which should give you time to recover your senses. And I will make sure that Valerie Marsh returns to England.'

She glanced across at Anna's downcast eyes and drooping mouth. Pity. They had all grown fond of the English girl, and Olga would be particularly upset at losing her. But young females were easily infatuated by a man's deep voice and penetrating eyes, and Valerie Marsh had obviously succumbed to the warmth and kindness of their Friend.

Such a susceptible creature would have to go. There was no knowing what trouble she might cause in the future, and the man of God was of far more importance to the Imperial family.

'She was only supposed to come here for one year,' said the Empress firmly, 'and it will be best if she returns home now to her own land and people. You may go.' She inclined her head towards the young officer.

Bowing again, Pyotr retreated. As he reached the far hallway, a voice called his name and, looking up, he saw Grand Duchess Olga on the landing above leaning over the white railings.

'Count Silakov, can you spare a minute? I am anxious about Valerie.' Olga's wide brow was furrowed in thought. 'Do you know where she is?'

'Yes,' he said, making no move to ascend, 'I know what has happened to Valerie Marsh and have just informed the Empress of the facts. She was most wickedly assaulted by Grigorii Rasputin, and is now recovering at the house of the Lees in St Petersburg.'

He heard Olga gasp, but ignored her.

'I have been ordered to go away from here and Valerie is to be sent back to England. Good day to you, Your Imperial Highness.'

He gave a swift bow then turned and ran across the hallway and out into the huge courtyard.

Let Olga and her mother sort out their differences with the help of that silly female, Anna Vyrubova. He wanted no more of them for a while, and Valerie would also be better off without them and their insane devotion to the Siberian peasant.

Mavara. The thought came to him with a sudden surge of relief as he strode towards the stables. He would send Tassya and Valerie to the gentler, friendlier south.

Unless, of course, Valerie preferred to return to England? But Pyotr did not believe she would. She and Tassya got on well together, Valerie could help his sister with his ailing mother's demands, and continue to improve her Russian at the same time.

Then he would spend this week with Sophia, discussing and planning their wedding.

★ ★ ★

Once Valerie had been bathed and dressed in a clean cotton night-gown, very voluminous and provided by Mrs Lees, she was put to bed by Katia, and fell instantly asleep. She was not aware of the Englishwoman tiptoeing into her chamber later that evening, nor of Katia's attempts to give her a glass of hot chocolate.

'Never mind,' said Mrs Lees, bending over the sleeping girl, 'we will leave her now. I'm sure sleep will be the best medicine. But stay with her, Katia, do not leave her alone, and I will come and see her in the morning,'

Katia huddled in the armchair all night long, but Valerie did not stir until late the following day when the bright spring sunshine filtered in through the drawn curtains.

Where on earth was she? It took her some minutes to realise she was once again in the bedroom she had occupied at Christmas, the pretty room with windows overlooking the Neva River in St. Petersburg — home of Mr and Mrs Lees. But what was she doing there?

As she sat up, pushing back her tousled hair, a maid-servant moved quickly to her side.

'Would you like some breakfast, bárishna?' asked Katia, thinking how much better the English girl looked after a good night's sleep.

'I would love some coffee and some brioches, please. But what am I doing here? And what is your name?'

Valerie didn't remember the maid from her

last visit, but then the Lees, like all the other affluent people in the capital, possessed many servants.

'I am Katia,' said the maid-servant, bobbing a curtsey, 'and you were brought here yesterday by an officer from the Imperial Guard, bárishna.'

Katia had noticed the foreigner's bruised lips and marks on her neck and breasts, and had also smelt the wine on her breath. And she had assumed that the girl had taken part in some amusement for the soldiers.

Pyotr. Immediately Valerie's mind began to function properly and she remembered his arms about her, and the joy of seeing him again, and the safety and happiness she had felt in his presence.

Then she remembered Rasputin and the terrible hours spent in his apartment, and the awful female disciples who had disregarded her cries for help and had even *envied* her being chosen by that monstrous man.

'Nothing to eat,' she said quickly, putting a hand to her mouth. 'Just some coffee, please, black and strong.'

Katia curtsied again and hurried from the room. The English girl had gone deathly pale, with all the pink in her cheeks draining away and leaving her face the same bleached white as the sheets.

What had happened to her? Memories were certainly causing her distress today. But Katia had little sympathy for the newcomer. They were all the same, the gentry. Too much money, too much food and drink, and every luxury and comfort provided for them by the workers.

As Katia was carrying the tray upstairs, Mrs Lees met her on the landing and enquired about Valerie.

'She is awake now? Thank goodness. I will take the tray and see to Miss Marsh myself, Katia. Go and assist Anna in my bedroom.'

Katia handed the tray to her mistress before going to join the other servant, and Mrs Lees took the coffee through to Valerie.

'I am so glad you are feeling more yourself, dear,' she said, setting the tray down on the bedside table, then perching on the edge of the bed and studying the girl.

Valerie was still very pale and her hair looked dreadful. Katia couldn't have washed it last night. But at least she smelt fresher and her nightgown was clean.

'Did you sleep well?' she asked, hoping to hear what had happened in the Siberian peasant's apartment.

But Valerie didn't want to talk. She couldn't force herself to speak of those terrible memories. As she poured a cup of welcome coffee and began to sip the hot liquid, she wished Pyotr would come and take her away once more.

She didn't want to stay with the Lees, she wanted to forget all about St Petersburg. She didn't even want to return to Tsarskoe Selo and the Imperial family. They had deceived her by their love and trust for that wicked man.

Suddenly she, too, thought of Mavara and the peace and calm of that oasis in the middle of the steppes. If Pyotr would only come and take her back there, she would gladly become his mistress and not care what *anybody* thought of her behaviour.

'Valerie, are you all right?' Mrs Lees was leaning forward, frowning. 'Do say something, dear. You have given us all a dreadful fright and I must know how you feel. Is there anything you wish to tell me, dear? I shall have to write to your father, but really do not know what to say to him until you speak to me.'

Valerie was not sure how much Mrs Lees had seen or heard the night before, but she was determined not to tell her anything more today.

'I am feeling better, thank you,' she said slowly, 'and am sorry to have caused you anxiety, Mrs Lees.' She wanted to leave the house, but where were her clothes? 'Is Count Silakov here?' She put a hand to her brow. 'I can't remember how I got here. Did you invite me, Mrs Lees?'

If she rolled her eyes and continued to look stupid, perhaps Mrs Lees would call for Pyotr to come and take her away. But she needed proper attire once she got out of bed. Where was her blouse, and skirt, and shoes?

'Do you remember nothing, Valerie?' Good heavens, the girl had lost her wits!

Valerie shook her head and gave a feeble smile.

'Are you going to accompany me back to England, Mrs Lees?'

This was intolerable. Mrs Lees tutted and rose to her feet.

'No, Valerie, we are not returning to England and Count Silakov went back to Tsarskoe Selo yesterday. He had to explain your absence to the Empress. Now I shall have to send a message to the palace and ask what is to be done with you.'

She walked out of the bedroom with her thoughts flying. As she hurried down the stairs she called for her husband, but Mr Lees had already left for the bank. So she would have to cope with this situation alone.

She would send the message to Anna Vyrubova and hope that she was readily available and would know how to contact the count.

Mrs Lees was vexed. Here she was with a girl who had lost her memory and her clothes; who had arrived in a sorry state at her house; had been dumped upon her, if the truth be told. And her husband had gone off as if nothing untoward had happened, leaving her alone with Valerie.

What if that peasant should arrive on her doorstep and demand the return of Valerie Marsh? What if he came rolling drunk up to her door and accosted *her*?

Mrs Lees' heart began beating hard against her whalebone stays. This sort of thing would never happen in their nice, refined residence in St John's Wood.

With trembling fingers Mrs Lees picked up her pen and began to write.

13

Mavara

Pyotr returned to Bolshoi Prospect as promised, and whisked Valerie away much to her own and Mrs Lees' relief. He brought some of her clothes and belongings with him, as well as a little note from Olga, which she had not yet read.

'You may go back to England, if you wish,' he said in the carriage, which took them to pick up Tassya at the Lukaev's mansion.

He was determined not to force her to do anything against her will. But he hoped very much that she would agree to going down to Mavara. She could help to care for his mother there, and would also be good company for Tassya. Dashka had been left at the palace. There were servants enough to assist Valerie at Mavara.

Fortunately Valerie agreed.

'There is nothing I would like more,' she said, looking at him with gratitude as the carriage travelled along Nevsky Prospect. 'I love your home and would love to help there. When will you come to join us?'

England held no appeal and she would think of something to tell her father. All she wanted now was to spend the rest of her life near Pyotr.

She would stay at Mavara until he came to join her, and then do whatever he asked of her. But during that time she was going to have a spring clean. She would roll up her sleeves and work as hard as any of the servants. It seemed that Countess Irina had to spend most of her time in bed so with both her and Tassya as semi-invalids, the house needed a strong healthy person to put it to rights.

Valerie was going to enjoy herself and she would be doing it all for the man she loved. 'Tassya believes I asked for your assistance because of Mother's ill-health,' said Pyotr. 'And as the Imperial family are always away during the summer months, I said they had granted you leave to help with Mother and Tassya.'

'What about Sophia?' asked Valerie. 'Does she know what happened?'

'Of course,' said Pyotr. 'It was Sophia who told me where you would be. Her maid, Vera, heard you and Tassya talking when you went to have tea there, and she told her mistress about your plans to visit Rasputin. You really have *her* to thank for your rescue.'

Now, standing at the open window of the compartment, looking down at Pyotr on the platform beneath her, Valerie knew everything was going to be all right. She had to accept Sophia in his life, but knew also that there would always be a small place for her in his heart,

'I will help at Mavara all I can,' she said, smiling down into his brilliant eyes.

And Pyotr, seeing her framed in the open window, small and soft and dove-like in her faded grey-blue travelling suit, realised she had recovered from her recent shock. Now that she was in the cheerful company of Tassya, she was beginning to blossom into the fresh and pretty Varinka he had known previously.

The red plush seats of their compartment folded down at night making two beds, and Dunya had been provided with a rug so she could sleep on the floor between them. There was a little room at the far end, which contained a basin with hot and cold water, and a closet, and Pyotr felt the girls were sure of every comfort.

'When will you be coming to join us?' asked Valerie, hoping it would not be too long before she saw him again.

'I am not quite sure at present,' said Pyotr. Much would depend on Sophia and the date she chose for their wedding.

'We will manage quite well without you, brother,' said Tassya, smiling at him through the glass and hoping he wouldn't come down too speedily. She needed time to exercise her slow old feet and a couple of weeks was not long enough. 'Come for my birthday,' she said.

'But that is months away,' said Valerie, frowning. 'Your mother will want to see you sooner than that, Pyotr.' So will I, she thought, but she couldn't say that.

'If mother is ill she will be thinking only of herself,' said Tassya, a little waspishly.

'Now, now.' Pyotr moved closer to the window and gave the glass by his sister's face a little tap. 'Be patient with Mother, and tell her I shall come home as soon as I can.'

Tassya nodded as her eyes began to sparkle. How she longed to tell her brother about her improvement. But Pyotr was not yet ready to believe in the holy man and she had the strangest feeling that Valerie, too, had turned against Father Grigorii.

Never mind, thought Tassya, waving as the train began moving slowly out of the station. She and Valerie hadn't had much time to themselves and she obviously couldn't speak about the holy man in Pyotr's presence. But now they were going to have days together in the train, and she would be able to ask Valerie everything she wanted to know.

Valerie, refreshed by two nights of unbroken slumber at the Lees, and thankful to be away from the curious banker's wife, wanted only to think about the future. To think about Mavara, and Pyotr's eventual coming. She wanted to organize the best cleaning and scrubbing, dusting and polishing, the tired old house had ever experienced. And it would keep her happily occupied whilst she waited.

But with Tassya's eager face in front of her, she was suddenly aware of the difficulties confronting her in the confined space they now shared. With all the chaos and upheaval of the past days, she had forgotten all about Tassya's connection with the Siberian peasant, and her innocent trust in him.

Oh heavens, how was she going to explain her revulsion of the man?

'Valerie, talk to me.' Tassya's voice was raised above the rhythmic pounding of the wheels as they rolled along the metal tracks. 'What did my holy man say to you? What did you say to him? Did you thank him properly for what he is doing for me?'

'I was trying to forget about that,' said Valerie slowly.

'What? I don't understand.' Tassya was impatient. What was wrong with Valerie? She wasn't a bit like the cheerful girl who had come to tea at the Lukaev's mansion. 'Come on — I want to know all about your visit.'

I'll have to tell her, thought Valerie, but it will break her heart. Perhaps the details could be watered down? Perhaps she could leave out the worst bits and pretend Rasputin had been playing a game?

Yet memories were so devastating she knew she couldn't lie.

Carefully Valerie began explaining about her arrival at the apartment and her surprise at finding so many Society ladies there, and how she had tried to leave and return another day.

Tassya nodded. 'I wouldn't have liked lots of people there,' she agreed, smiling as she remembered the quiet antechamber and the calm, reassuring presence of the man of God. 'It was just Dunya and I when we were there, and the sound of his wonderful deep voice praying over me.'

Valerie sighed. How could she make Tassya understand that there were two Rasputins? One, a good man who worked miracles. But also another, who enjoyed bedding as many different females as he could.

'Let's leave it, Tassya,' she said. 'You remember a holy man and I remember a very different being.'

'But you can't leave it like that,' said Tassya, frowning across at Valerie. 'What is the matter with you? How can I understand your strange attitude if you don't tell me what happened?'

'Very well,' said Valerie stiffly. 'All the ladies were drunk and forced me to drink too much wine. Rasputin was also drunk. Then I was dragged into his bedroom against my will and two of the women undressed me.'

Tassya gasped, staring at Valerie with huge eyes.

'Then that awful man came in and told the others to go. He lay down on the bed with me and wouldn't let me go. He was smelly and hairy and revolting.' Valerie fumbled for her handkerchief. 'It was dreadful, Tassya, and I hate him!'

'You are lying,' said Tassya, her cheeks aflame. 'My man of God would never do anything like that!'

Dunya, who was sitting in the far corner, stood up and went to sit beside her mistress. She put an arm around Tassya's shoulders and spoke softly to her.

'It is the truth,' said Valerie, wiping her face. 'How I wish it was not. Then Pyotr came and rescued me, thank God.'

Tassya shook off Dunya's arm and glared. This foreign girl, whom she had thought was her friend, was trying to destroy two of the most important things in her life. Her blessed healer, Father Grigorii, and her faith in him.

'I don't believe the Imperial family allowed you to come here on leave,' she said suddenly. 'I believe they have dismissed you. They love Father Grigorii just as I do, and they don't want you around spreading wicked lies about him, Valerie Marsh.'

Valerie shrugged and turned her head to look out of the window. It was useless trying to convince Tassya so she would keep quiet and think about Pyotr. *He* knew the truth, and would support and comfort her when he came south.

Tassya also remained silent, but her mind was filling with dislike for this English girl whose lies had so upset her.

★ ★ ★

When they first arrived at Mavara, Tassya insisted on being at her mother's bed all day long, so Valerie was sent to fetch and carry for both of them.

She had to take messages down to the kitchen, tell Sidor Novatko what to prepare for each meal, and give the maids their orders. There was no spring clean as she had

213

imagined it, but a continual running to and fro up and down stairs.

'Tell Sidor there was too much salt in the borscht last night. I could not drink it,' said Countess Irina.

And —

'Go and see Feodor about these lamps. The wicks are too low and they smell abominably.'

And 'Go to the linen room, Valerie, and look me out some better sheets. Then tell Galina to take more care with her sewing. Mine have been badly mended and I cannot sleep on them.'

All the while Tassya sat composedly beside her mother, looking as contented as a well-fed cat. And Dunya, sewing some unimportant item, would glance up with an equally satisfied air. There were three other maid servants in the house, but none of them was ever called once Valerie arrived at Mavara.

Valerie thought Countess Irina looked older and more haggard than when she had last seen her and, although the woman did not complain of pain her doctor had said rest, so rest she did.

She had lost weight and sat scarecrow-like, her yellow face against the pillows, but her brown eyes were still sharp and her voice harsh.

To begin with, Tassya had read to her mother and written letters for her, whilst Valerie had run errands for them both and carried trays up to the first floor for their meals three times a day. But quite soon Tassya had become bored in the sick-room and eager to distance herself from such an irritable and demanding patient.

'Pyotr sent you down here to help us,' she told Valerie, when her mother was taking her afternoon nap, 'and as I need Dunya to help more with my legs *you* must stay with Mother and do whatever she wants.'

Valerie, who was beginning to wish she had brought Dashka with her, was thankful to agree. She enjoyed reading and writing letters, and the thought of sitting for longer periods was pleasing. She would also hear all Pyotr's news and be able to write to him in his mother's name.

Unfortunately she had forgotten about the Cyrillic alphabet. Although her knowledge of spoken Russian had improved considerably, she had no idea how to write the language.

This didn't affect her reading as the countess was very fond of both Dickens and Jane Austen, and possessed sets of both authors' works printed in English. But Valerie knew she could never cope with any correspondence.

However the countess soon had a solution to that problem.

'I am quite capable of reading my own letters,' she said, 'but do not intend labouring over the replies. So you write them your way, Valerie, and I will spell the words for you. We are not all illiterate peasants here, you know. And those with whom I wish to correspond will be quite capable of understanding — so long as your script is legible.'

Valerie learned when Pyotr returned to Tsarskoe Selo and resumed his duties, although there was no mention of the Empress. So in the next letter from the countess to her son, Valerie slipped in a note addressed to Grand Duchess Olga, thanking her for hers.

Soon after arriving at Mavara she had found the courage to read Olga's letter, which Pyotr had given her in St Petersburg. To her relief the words, although short and stilted, showed she didn't hate Valerie for what had happened.

' . . . I was very sorry to hear such bad news of you, Valerie — I wish we could talk, but perhaps it is just as well if you go south. Time heals all wounds and maybe before too long we will meet again. I shall miss you. Olga Nicolaievna.'

There was sympathy in the letter despite its

brevity and that helped Valerie during her days of drudgery in the crumbling old house, as well as her thoughts of Pyotr.

To add to her discomfort, she had been made to realize very early on that the other servants disliked taking orders from a foreigner, even though the words stemmed from Countess Irina. She was hurt by their looks of scorn, or scarcely-concealed sniggers as she struggled with yet another embarrassing demand, or reprimand, from on high.

Even Feodor, though more dignified in his behaviour, showed by his raised eyebrows, or by making her repeat a message, that Valerie was not his mistress, nor acceptable in the household where she was no longer a guest.

So all she could do was grit her teeth and wait for Pyotr to come and tell her what the future held for them both.

14

'May I join you, Varinka?'

Valerie's head jerked up from her sewing and she lay down her needlework as she saw Pyotr standing in the open doorway.

'Oh, please come in — I've wanted to talk to you for days, but we never get the chance to be on our own together.' She held out her hands to the tall, dark-haired man who came loping towards her, looking cool and wonderfully fit in his loose cotton trousers and blue peasant's blouse. 'Where are the others?' she whispered, as he cupped her face in his warm hands and silenced her with a kiss.

As Valerie fondled his springy thick hair and felt his mouth on hers, she rejoiced at the clean masculine smell of him. It had been so long since she had been in his arms, she couldn't get enough of his kisses and hard body close to hers.

Pyotr, in turn, savoured her sweetness, revelling in her soft receptive lips and smoothing her tender body with his hands, Then he raised his mouth from hers and pulled her to her feet, before seating himself on the chair and drawing her back to lean against him.

'Sophia and Tassya have gone to Kamenka for yet more shopping, and as Mother is sound asleep next door I felt this was the best time for us to talk, my love. But why so thin, Varinka?'

He had seen little of her since arriving at Mavara, for Tassya always joined him and Sophia at mealtimes, whilst Valerie remained upstairs with his mother. Even when he went to talk to the countess Valerie was scarcely visible, sitting on a chair by the window saying nothing unless spoken to. But what could he say when his mother was always present?

'I have been working quite hard,' Valerie said, rubbing her cheek against the light cotton of his blouse, almost purring as his right hand slid down the open neck of her dress and began caressing one small breast.

'Even these are thinner,' he grumbled, lowering his head to nibble at her neck then at the smooth milky whiteness of her breast.

'You must not!' She was almost whimpering with longing for him to remove her clothing and allow him to kiss and fondle every part of her quivering body. 'Your mother will wake up soon and I must be ready to go to her.'

Slowly he lifted his head to place his face against her shiny hair, but his hand stayed inside her bodice cupping her flesh, his fingers playing with her nipple.

'You have been working like a slave, have you not, Varinka? Was it by your choice, or did my womenfolk insist upon such grudging?'

'Grudging?' Valerie stared. Then she burst out laughing. 'You mean drudgery, Pyotr Silakov! Your English is not improving I fear.' She removed his hand from inside her dress and kissed it. 'I don't mind the work, but I hated it at first and it was only thoughts of you that kept me going.'

Then she turned and looked down at him with such longing, such tenderness in her pale face, that Pyotr felt a stab of self-loathing pierce his body. If only he could have married *this* girl!

'You won't ever leave me, will you, Petya? I know your wife and children must always come first, but you won't forget your Varinka?'

He stood up and drew her close in one last desperate embrace.

'I will never leave you, my dearest one. Just be patient for a while longer,' he said. 'Sophia and I will tell Mother of our betrothal this evening and that news will invigorate her as well as Mavara.' He smiled briefly. 'Then we will come down to celebrate Tassya's birthday in August and hopefully our marriage date will be settled by then. Once that is done I shall be able to plan a future for you, my love.'

'Not till then?'

August seemed very far away. Why was she not independent and able to leave Mavara and set up her own home elsewhere? Valerie was acutely aware of her dire need of Pyotr, not only physically, but also financially. Without him she was nothing.

Looking across at him standing in the doorway about to depart, she knew she loved him most ardently. But she was not the only female in his life and had to accept that she was the least important.

Sophia possessed the essential wealth, Countess Irina would have to be cared for and her feelings considered until she died, and Tassya would be her brother's responsibility unless, or until, she married.

Pyotr's mistress, however desirable, would never have a real claim on him.

Quickly she forced herself to think about the countess as Pyotr left her alone. Countess Irina needed her and in some strange way she was beginning to like the woman. As Tassya had withdrawn more and more from their company, Valerie had grown closer to the invalid.

The old woman never showed gratitude for what Valerie did, but they shared the same taste in literature and, although the countess snapped at her pronunciation, Valerie knew that her knowledge of Russian was improving rapidly during their sessions together.

So patience was all that mattered now. Patience, and complete trust in Pyotr.

★　★　★

That evening after dinner they all went through to the big salon at the rear of the house, where Sophia had once played the piano so beautifully and where Valerie, clad in Grand Duchess Olga's apple-green satin gown, had last danced with Pyotr.

Valerie almost smiled, thinking of her changed circumstances. She was wearing her usual drab grey, more worn and faded than during her time with the Imperial family. Because her two day dresses were in constant use, and she was without the funds to pay for new material, her poor grey and blue cottons would have to last the summer.

Fleetingly she wondered what had become of the muslins and laces that had been made for her in the Crimea. But Pyotr had been in such a hurry collecting her belongings from Alexander Palace, it was not surprising that many items had been left behind.

However, the other younger females graced the salon with elegance and style. Tassya in the prettiest of white muslins, which had recently been given to her by Sophia. It had an emerald green ribbon threaded through her round neckline and short puffed sleeves.

Valerie had noticed that Sophia wore a different dress both daytime and evenings, and was now wearing wine red taffeta with pearls at her throat and a rope of them entwined in her high piled lustrous black hair.

The countess reclined on a chaise-longue, which had been given to her by Sophia. It was set in the middle of the bare floorboards whilst the other chairs were placed in a semicircle in front of her. Her sallow face was flushed with pleasure and she clutched a small velvet box over the rug on her knees.

It was a warm evening and the glass doors had been opened onto the verandah, but Pyotr's mother seemed to feel cold and told Valerie to run and fetch her shawl.

Pyotr frowned at this command and glanced towards Dunya, as if to order her upstairs, but at that precise moment Tassya turned her head to say something to her maid, who was standing behind her chair.

So Valerie left the room without demur.

'This has been in the Silakov family for over one hundred years,' the countess was saying, as she returned. 'And I am proud to pass it on to you, Sophia Lukaev.'

Valerie placed the shawl around the old woman's shoulders and saw that the box now lay open, lined with gold satin, and holding a cabuchon ruby set in pearls, on a platinum ring.

'Here, Petya,' said the countess, 'place it on her finger. Wear it with pride, Sophia, and when your first son becomes engaged to marry, you must give it to him for *his* bride. Thus it will continue in the family.'

'I will.' Sophia smiled as Pyotr slid the magnificent ruby onto her finger.

Valerie looked away as he bent to kiss his betrothed, trying to show no emotion as she settled down next to Tassya's wheelchair.

'When is the wedding to be?' asked Tassya. 'It must not be before my birthday, Petya. My celebration must come first!'

She was laughing as she gave her head an imperious little nod, the green velvet ribbon holding back her dark curls.

'Probably in the autumn,' said Sophia, glancing at Pyotr. 'But there is much to be altered and improved here, Tassya, before I can set foot in my new home.'

'Altered?' Countess Irina looked across at the glowing, wine-red beauty with her ruby ring, uncertain what was meant by that remark. She did not like change and would not tolerate any upheaval in her life. 'What do you intend on doing, Sophia?'

'It will all be for the better,' said Sophia soothingly.

Valerie hoped she would not be there.

'The west wing will remain more or less as it is now,' said Sophia, 'although the kitchen needs painting and re-organizing. But the east wing is going to be re-opened and the rooms made ready for all the visitors we intend having. That is agreed, isn't it, Petya?'

Pyotr nodded.

'You will have your own suite of rooms,' Sophia went on, patting the countess's hand. 'There are many upstairs that have been unused for years. So Pyotr and I will have our apartment across the centre, where the linen room and your present room are now, and you will have rooms in the west wing leaving the upstairs of the other wing for our children.'

Her yellow eyes were ablaze with excitement as she saw Mavara as she envisaged it — with Chinese wallpaper, and Persian carpets and elegant walnut furniture throughout the many rooms.

'There is so much space,' said Sophia. 'It just needs filling with beautiful objects.'

Tassya was frowning. 'What about me?' she said. Her home was about to change before her eyes and, like her mother, she was not sure she liked the idea.

'There are several rooms along that west wing, aren't there, Tassya?' Sophia turned her attention to the girl in the wheelchair. She was Pyotr's sister and must not be left out of these splendid arrangements. 'We will go and look tomorrow, dear, and I'll tell you what I have in mind.'

'What about Valerie Marsh then,' said Tassya, drawing everyone's attention to the startled girl, who had been contemplating her moments of approaching happiness with Pyotr.

'Valerie must return to England,' said Sophia quickly. 'Don't you agree, Petya?'

'I think it would be polite to ask Valerie what *she* would like,' said Pyotr. 'She was invited to Russia by the Romanovs and, when she was no longer needed by them, I invited her to Mavara. What would you like to do, Valerie?'

For one dreadful moment Valerie didn't know how to reply.

'Everything has happened so suddenly,' she said slowly, 'I need some time to think things through.'

'Nonsense!' said the countess, rearranging the shawl around her shoulders. 'There is no question of Valerie leaving here whilst I am alive. I need the girl, Pyotr, and find her a surprisingly useful companion. Quite intelligent for a foreigner,' she said, her black eyes glittering, 'and I cannot do without her. Make your arrangements, Sophia. Do what you will with my old home. But make sure of an extra room in my suite. Valerie Marsh remains with me.'

'I think it would be best if we allowed matters to drop for this evening,' said Pyotr, with a reassuring nod at Valerie.

Some time tonight he would go to Valerie's room and talk to her. Tomorrow she would have to announce her intentions for the future.

'Let us all have a good night's rest,' he went on, 'and Valerie can tell us her plans in the morning.'

'Very well,' said Sophia.

Perhaps it would be a good idea if the foreigner remained at Mavara. Sophia was not sure she could tolerate her domineering mother-in-law even in her invalid state. And Valerie Marsh had been useful up till now. In the morning she would tell Pyotr that the English girl could stay.

★ ★ ★

That night Countess Irina was restless, worrying over the possibility of Valerie's departure, and all the changes about to take place in her home.

After being woken on three different occasions, Valerie carried her bedding through and placed it on the floor in the old woman's chamber. Exactly like a serving-maid, she thought ruefully, but her presence seemed to soothe the countess and she was not disturbed again that night.

However, being in that other room she was unaware of Pyotr's attempts to see her. Nor did she get the chance to speak to him again as Sophia was constantly with him.

But she did manage to comfort the countess by saying she had decided to remain with her for the time being.

On the morning of Pyotr's departure with his betrothed, Sophia was dazzling in white lace with a straw hat decorated with blood red roses, and with rubies in her ears and the huge ruby on her finger. She looked so radiant that Valerie hoped fiercely that they hadn't slept together.

Once Pyotr and Sophia were man and wife, she would have to accept their conjugal state. But the thought that they had already consummated their union was intolerable.

You had the chance, she told herself grimly, plumping up the pillows behind the countess's back as if they were Sophia's body, and you prudishly barred the door against him. Now she wished she had given in to Pyotr's demands and enjoyed a few nights of bliss with her love.

But such thoughts were useless. All she could do now was wait at Mavara for Pyotr to come and tell her what to do.

★   ★   ★

The next weeks passed so quickly with workmen arriving and transforming the house into Sophia's dream palace, that Valerie had little time to ponder her future.

Pyotr did not come down again until just before Tassya's birthday, but Sophia came and went at unexpected intervals, making sure that the work was progressing to her satisfaction.

Early in July she arrived with news that had not yet reached Mavara.

'Haven't you heard?' she said, taking off her wide straw hat which was decorated with red cherries this time, and flinging it on the floor as she collapsed onto the new Regency-striped sofa in the pink salon.

This room was at last completed and, because the weather was unpleasantly hot, Valerie and the countess and Tassya had all thankfully retired to the room at the rear of the house to greet their visitor.

'Archduke Franz Ferdinand has been shot by a young Serb in Sarajevo, and Austria is furious!' Sophia was enjoying the looks of bewilderment on the faces before her. 'Has Pyotr not written to tell you, madam?'

Countess Irina shook her head. 'No doubt I shall hear from him this week but that news is worrying. Is the Archduke dead?'

Sophia nodded.

'Why is it worrying, Mama?' Tassya gazed across at her mother looking bright and perky in strawberry pink cotton.

She was walking quite well now and had almost told her mother yesterday. But her plan was to inform them all on her seventeenth birthday, and she was not going to spoil the surprise. There were only three more weeks to go so she could be patient a while longer.

'Why does it matter what Austria is thinking?' she said.

Valerie, too, sensed the old woman's

concern, but had only a vague idea who Archduke Ferdinand was, and none at all about a Serb. What a strange name.

'Because, you ignorant child, the Serbs are all Slavs and detest being ruled by two non-Slavic races — the Austrians and the Magyars of Hungary,' said the countess.

'And Franz Ferdinand was assassinated because he was Austrian,' said Sophia. She leaned back against the pink and silver striped cushions and sighed. 'Heavens, but it's hot outside!'

'His uncle, Franz Joseph, is the Emperor,' said the countess, 'but he is an old man and his nephew was going to inherit the throne of the massive Austro-Hungarian Empire.'

Valerie was very aware of her lack of education but, like Tassya, wondered why this assassination should be so important to the outside world.

'What will happen now?' asked Tassya, looking at her mother. But it was Sophia who replied.

'The Austrians are insisting it is Serbia's declaration of war on Austria-Hungary,' she said. 'And Petersburg is fairly humming with talk of war.'

'But it cannot possibly affect *us*!' said Tassya.

If war came to Russia it would mean

Andrei Odarka going into battle, and she had planned such a wonderful surprise for him. Pyotr had promised to bring his friend down to Mavara for her birthday party, so there *couldn't* be a war to spoil everything!

'We won't go to war,' said Sophia. 'This has nothing to do with Russia.'

Valerie felt sick. If war came, Pyotr would be sent to the front and what if he should die? Why was Sophia looking so calm? Didn't she care about her betrothed?

'Russia is the traditional protector of the Slavs,' said the countess hoarsely. 'If Serbia asks for our help I am certain Tsar Nicholas will have to offer assistance.'

'It won't come to war,' said Sophia firmly. 'Pyotr says the Tsar will never agree. We are not prepared and besides, a tiny kingdom like Serbia is not worth fighting for.'

'I hope he is right,' said the countess, looking at her future daughter-in-law with speculative eyes. 'Tell me, how is my son?'

'He is very well,' said Sophia, smiling and fingering the ruby on her hand. 'He will be coming down with Andrei for Tassya's birthday, and sends his love, madam. Let us hope the weather will have cooled down by then. I came away from Petersburg to escape the heat, but find it even hotter down here.'

Rising gracefully to her feet, Sophia walked

across to the fireplace to ring the bell set in the wall beside the pink marble surround. The grate had been cleared of ashes and scrubbed clean. She frowned as she studied the empty space.

When Feodor entered in answer to her ring, Sophia told him to tell her maid-servant to bring a fan.

'And we need a great vase of flowers, Feodor, a crystal vase,' she said, 'and masses of blooms. Have them picked and sent in at once.'

Behind her the countess chuckled.

'You'll get no blooms in this heat, Sophia. A few geraniums, perhaps, but they are the only flowers surviving in the garden and Conrad told me yesterday that all the water barrels are empty.' She seemed to find pleasure in thwarting the younger woman's extravagance.

'Then I shall have flowers sent here from town. It is only a matter of organization, Countess Irina.'

'And finance,' put in the other swiftly.

'Water can be brought up from the lake — I presume *that* has not run dry?' said Sophia.

At that moment Vera arrived with a white lace fan, which she handed to her mistress. As Sophia began to fan her face Valerie wondered if the unusual red of her cheeks was caused by the heat, or by annoyance at the countess's words?

The weather remained oppressively hot and Valerie often remembered the Crimea, and those blissful weeks spent there with the Imperial family. Although that visit had been so much earlier in the year it had felt like summer down by the Black Sea, with the deliciously cool sea breezes, the light clothing they had worn and the lack of physical exertion.

At Livadia Palace, Valerie had not had to run up and down stairs obeying the demands of a querulous old woman, nor had she been confined for many hours to a hot and stuffy room.

She had suggested sitting outside on the verandah at the rear of the house, or beneath the huge mulberry tree that shaded a wide area of the yard. But Countess Irina preferred staying indoors.

She seemed to take pleasure in moaning about the hammering and banging of the workmen, as well as the discomfort of the one room that she and Valerie shared until the suite in the west wing was completed.

The countess only consented to being brought downstairs when Sophia came to visit, so for once Valerie looked forward to the beauty arriving at Mavara.

Tassya she seldom saw and Valerie regretted their continual enmity. She had tried talking to her, but Tassya no longer accepted her friendship and lived a secret life with Dunya downstairs.

When Sophia visited, Tassya showed interest in her company, like her mother, and the two appeared to get on well. But the moment Sophia returned to St Petersburg, Tassya withdrew once more into her private world.

Valerie was sure her legs were improving and remembered how Tassya had vowed to surprise them all on her birthday. If this small miracle did occur, perhaps Tassya would be friends with her again?

She missed Pyotr dreadfully and longed for his strong, masculine presence. If she were in his arms, hearing his loving voice, feeling his body against hers, she could face the world with confidence. But on her own in this dusty, noisy, house with only the company of an ailing embittered woman, Valerie was continually fearful.

What would happen if war came to Russia? What would she do if Pyotr was sent away to the front and she was left at Mavara with Tassya and Sophia and Countess Irina? What would become of her if he should die?

15

At the end of July Pyotr returned accompanied by Sophia and Andrei Odarka, as he had promised his sister.

When the group from St Petersburg arrived at Mavara, Valerie was overjoyed to see his tall figure leaping down from the carriage. Both he and Andrei were still wearing their white summer uniforms with gold buttons and braid and epaulettes glinting in the sunshine. But as they were eager to change into light attire, they went swiftly to their rooms promising to join the ladies shortly on the verandah.

Conrad had met them at Kamenka railway station and he and Feodor helped to carry the luggage upstairs. Vera went with them to see to her mistress's unpacking and Sophia joined the countess and Valerie on the verandah.

She looked fresh and lovely in a cream muslin frock edged with honey-coloured lace. Her shiny black hair was curled into ringlets reaching to her shoulders, and her wide-brimmed straw hat sported a honey-coloured ribbon with a bunch of velvet primroses clustering on its brim.

Was this the same straw hat redecorated to match each outfit? Or did Sophia possess as many different hats as she did dresses? Valerie could not control a twinge of envy.

'It is good to be down here again,' said Sophia, walking along the verandah to peck at Countess Irina's cheek, then sitting beside her on one of the cane chairs. 'After we have had tea I shall have a look around. I hope the men have almost finished now.'

The countess's suite of rooms was complete and she and Valerie had moved into the west wing to space and comfort. They had a bedroom each, linked by a sitting room decorated in apricot and leaf green, and a small bathroom next to the countess's room.

Despite all this indulgence, however, Countess Irina was not happy. Tucked away over the west wing she felt isolated and no longer part of the household.

'We will need more servants,' she said. 'Feodor cannot manage with so many extra rooms to clean, and Valerie has much further to walk with our meals and the errands she does for me.'

Valerie's heart lifted in gratitude. So the countess *had* noticed what she did.

'We will employ many more servants, do not worry, dear madam,' said Sophia.

At that moment Tassya was wheeled through the open glass doors by Dunya, and her chair placed beside Sophia's. Valerie was at the end of the verandah, but she didn't mind the far corner as it allowed her a good view of everyone else.

Tassya had insisted on being rushed away when the noise of arrival had been heard in the courtyard. She wanted to make sure her hair was neat and she looked pretty for Andrei. Tomorrow was The Day and she could scarcely wait to show them what she had achieved. All due to Father Grigorii. Then Valerie would have to acknowledge that he was a true man of God, and her brother and Sophia would realize he was a miraculous healer.

Valerie, looking at Tassya's crisp lavender-blue cotton frock, with matching ribbons in her hair, longed for another dress. A best one, which she could wear on special occasions like tomorrow. Even Countess Irina had asked for her faded, mushroom-coloured moiré to be brought out from the cupboard and made ready for her daughter's birthday.

All her hopes were pinned on Pyotr, and their future life together. But how could she ever see him alone?

The room she now occupied was reached through Countess Irina's bedroom and the

238

linking sitting room, so there could be no nocturnal visits from him unless he played Romeo and appeared at her window from the top of a ladder.

Tassya, who caught sight of Valerie's small smile, wondered what was passing through her mind? She shouldn't have secrets. This was Tassya's birthday and all the attention should be centred on her.

'We are having a picnic down by the lake tomorrow,' she announced loudly, 'and Mother is coming in the trap, and Conrad and Feodor and the other servants are bringing the cart filled with food and drink.'

'How nice,' said Sophia. 'But not during the day, Tassya, it will be far too hot.'

'In the evening.' Tassya nodded. 'And we'll fish for crayfish. Valerie, I hope you will join Dunya in her fishing. She is very good at it.'

Countess Irina tutted as her daughter burst out laughing.

'I will gladly help Dunya,' said Valerie, wondering what the hilarity was about. 'But she will have to show me what to do. I've never been fishing before.'

As Tassya roared with laughter again, joined this time by her maid, Pyotr and Andrei came out onto the verandah dressed in their light blouses and baggy trousers.

'What's all this merriment about?' asked

Pyotr, walking over to kiss his mother then moving round behind her cane chair and resting his hands on the back of it.

This way he was standing close to his betrothed, but could get a good look at Valerie at the same time. It was disconcerting to see that she had grown even thinner and appeared drawn in the face so that she looked much older than her nineteen years. Compared to the glamorous Sophia, his little Varinka was as worn and wrung out as an old dishcloth.

She needed money spent on her, he thought, new clothes, and a kinder way of life. Valerie Marsh was no servant, but a lady of quality. Yet here at Mavara her life had reached a very low ebb.

Pyotr frowned as he saw the same dress she had worn the last time he was there, and the same she had worn at Tsarskoe Selo. Well, he was going to do something about that now.

The marriage settlement had been finalised, both he and Sophia's parents had signed the various documents, and the date of their wedding had been planned for 17 September. The dowry money would be his after that date, but until then a small amount remained in his bank and he was going to make sure that Valerie received enough to keep her going until the autumn.

Andrei could escort Sophia back to St Petersburg whilst he stayed on in the Ukraine for a few more days. He would go over all the finances of the estate with his mother and, at the same time, find a suitable abode for his Varinka.

Valerie, watching Pyotr's face, saw the light of triumph in his eyes and caught her breath. Your future is secure, my love, he was telling her. Trust me. And she could have shouted aloud with relief and delight.

'Our laughter, dearest brother, was about the cray-fishing tomorrow,' said Tassya. 'Valerie is going to help Dunya with her catch. Is that not amusing?' She was giggling again, eager to gain his support.

'Help Dunya?' For a moment Pyotr stared in amazement, first at his sister, then at her maid. 'Did you hear that, Mother?'

He turned his gaze on the countess and walked round to sit on the end of her cane couch. 'Did you know what she intended?' His eyes were ablaze with anger.

'Gracious me, what is this all about?' Sophia was as surprised as Valerie by the sudden air of tension on the verandah.

'I would not have allowed it,' said the countess, stretching out to touch Pyotr's hand, which was clenched tightly on his knee. 'It was only a joke, Petya. Tassya is becoming a little over-excited about her birthday.'

'Over-excited? I call it downright rude.' He glared at his sister, whose giggles had faded to a pout.

'It would have been fun to watch, Petya, especially for you and Andrei,' she said.

'Valerie is not a servant, Tassya. Although by the look of her, and by the way you and Mother have behaved towards her, she seems to have been treated exactly like one,' said Pyotr.

'For goodness sake stop this bickering and tell me what this cray-fishing is all about!' Sophia closed her fan with a sharp click then reached forward to hit Pyotr's thigh with a light downward stroke. 'Tell me, Pyotr Silakov!'

Valerie stared, surprised by the antagonism between brother and sister, and the confusion of Countess Irina. She was grateful to Pyotr for coming to her aid, but cray-fishing seemed a very mild activity compared to what she normally did every day.

'Years ago,' said Pyotr shortly, looking at Sophia, 'when we were much younger, Dunya used to go into the lake naked and search for crayfish lying in the mud at the bottom.'

'And I thought you would enjoy that also, Valerie,' said Tassya. 'You told me once you couldn't swim so think how cool and refreshing the water would be on your hot body.'

The blood rushed to Valerie's face. This was another way of punishing her for what she had said about Tassya's adored Father Grigorii.

'I didn't realize that such a childish prank was your idea of party entertainment, Tassya,' she said. 'But I am grateful to Pyotr for enlightening me and will not be accompanying you tomorrow, Countess Irina,' she told the flustered woman.

'Now, now, Valerie, do not take offence,' said the countess, leaning back in her seat and placing a hand on her palpitating bosom. 'It was a naughty thing for Tassya to say, but no harm was intended. I cannot possibly manage without you and *of course* you must come to the picnic. It is a special day for my daughter and we must *all* go down to the lake and celebrate with her.'

'Sorry, Valerie,' said Tassya quickly. Once they had raised their glasses to toast her, she intended flinging back the rug and stepping out of her chair. What a sensation that would be! And she wanted as big an audience as possible to witness the miracle. 'You must come, Valerie. Mother is quite right and I apologize for offending you. But it was only meant as a joke.'

'I think it should be a double celebration,' said Andrei suddenly. He, too, had found Tassya's plan offensive and wondered if he had been mistaken in thinking she was a sweet and innocent girl. Perhaps her disabled state had fostered a black side to her normally gentle nature? 'We must celebrate Tassya's birthday, of course, but we should also show our gratitude to Valerie for all she has done for the family these past months.'

'Hear! Hear!' said Pyotr, grinning at his friend and thankful that the praise had not come from his own lips.

Sophia frowned and Tassya sniffed, but remained silent. Andrei had not found her idea as amusing as she had hoped. Countess Irina, however, agreed wholeheartedly. She was not going to lose Valerie Marsh under any circumstances, so a little praise would not go amiss.

'That is settled then,' she said firmly. 'We will all go down to the lake tomorrow evening, and the cray-fishing will be done entirely with rods and nets.'

Everyone smiled at her words except Valerie. She would join the others and take part in Tassya's celebrations, and if they wished to praise her it would make a welcome change. But that did not detract one jot from her longing to get away and she prayed Pyotr would find a moment to seek her out. She wanted to know what he had in mind for them both. Perhaps tomorrow whilst the others were fishing, they would find a few minutes to speak to each other?

★ ★ ★

'What is happening at Tsarskoe Selo?' Countess Irina drew everybody's attention to a more ominous topic. 'Will Russia go to war, Petya?'

He shook his head. 'Austria has declared war on Serbia, and Tsar Nicholas has returned from his holiday on the Imperial yacht and summoned his ministers to the palace. He has also ordered all military districts along the Austrian border to be mobilized — '

'Then it *is* war!' cried the countess. 'Oh, my God, when do you go to the front, Petya?'

'Now, Mother,' he said, leaning forward and catching hold of her hands, 'do not get so agitated. It is not war, and the Tsar has only done this as a precautionary measure.'

'You didn't tell me,' said Sophia. 'You said everything was fine at Tsarskoe Selo.'

'And so it is,' said Pyotr. 'We are not prepared for war and have neither the rifles, nor the artillery, to take part in any major conflict.'

'Only the men,' said Andrei quietly.

'Oh, don't go *on* so!' Tassya's excitement had dwindled at the sight of so many long faces. 'Tomorrow is my birthday and we should be thinking about that and all the happy things in life — not war, and bloodshed, and destruction.'

Andrei, who had been leaning against the verandah railing, straightened his long body and went to stand beside her chair.

'We will have a splendid time tomorrow, little Tassya,' he said, placing his hands on her shoulders and bending to give her a quick hug. 'I cannot wait to see this surprise you have promised us. It is not Valerie Marsh cray-fishing, I presume?'

At once Tassya was smiling again.

'It is far more exciting than cray-fishing, Andrei.' She was elated by the affection in his voice, and by the warmth of his hands on her body.

But Valerie, who was watching her and Andrei, as well as Pyotr and Sophia opposite them, felt the cold fingers of premonition close around her heart. They were together, couples who belonged to each other. Whilst she was an outsider, who belonged to no-one.

Pyotr had promised never to leave her, and she believed him. However, if war came and he was sent to the front she would have no right to him as a wife, or mother, or sister would. She would not be informed if he were injured or, God forbid, killed.

She could wait for weeks and weeks knowing nothing and who would inform her? Whom would she dare to ask for news of him?

In peacetime she and Pyotr could make a love-nest for themselves and form a secretive yet enduring relationship that would last all their lives. But if war came to Russia, Valerie Marsh would be a nobody — a foreigner, without money, and without any claim on the man she loved.

Pyotr, glancing across at her strained face, guessed at what was passing through her mind and longed to hold her, to tell her that everything would be all right. I am yours now and forever and we will be together, I promise, my Varinka. Then Sophia's hand came down on his heavy with the weight of her ruby ring, and her voice drew his attention.

'Do you think we should bring the marriage day forward, dearest Petya? Perhaps we should marry early next month? If war *should* come, you will be called up at once and we might not be together on the 17 September?'

'There is no need to rush,' he said reassuringly.

All the necessary arrangements had been made in St Petersburg and he was not going to be forced into an earlier marriage. There was only one month to wait, after all, and a great deal to be organized before then. Like his mother, but for very different reasons, Pyotr was not going to lose Valerie. But time was needed in which to sort out her new abode.

★   ★   ★

'Do you think there is going to be a war, Andrei?' asked the countess, wanting another opinion, unsure what to think.

'I don't believe the Tsar wants war,' Andrei said carefully, 'but an attack on Serbia can only be interpreted as a challenge to Russia's power and her influence in the Balkans. We cannot stand by and allow Serbia to be humiliated. If we do, we will lose rank as a great power.'

'I think it all depends on Germany,' said Pyotr. 'If, as I hope, the Kaiser wants war as little as Tsar Nicholas, then the conflict can remain a small affair left to sort itself out. But if Germany goes to the aid of the Austro-Hungarian Empire, then I fear

Europe will become a battlefield.'

There was silence as they all absorbed his words.

'So we wait to hear what Kaiser Wilhelm decides,' said the countess eventually.

'Well, I'm off to bed,' said Sophia, bored by the politics and wanting the next day to come as quickly as possible. She had the most extravagant and beautiful outfit to wear.

It was French and wildly expensive, but she longed to see Pyotr's and Andrei's expressions when she paraded in it. It was not right for a picnic but was ideal for a celebration. And Tassya was not going to be the only one to receive attention.

'Good night,' she said, rising to her feet and smiling at the raised faces. 'I will see you all tomorrow.'

She bent to kiss Pyotr before he stood up, then walked through the open glass doors into her new pink salon. This was a glorious room and just one of the many changes taking place at Mavara. Soon it would be well and truly hers.

Sighing with satisfaction, Sophia Lukaev climbed the stairs to her bedroom.

16

Next day Pyotr managed to see Valerie on her own.

After a midday meal of pork and tomatoes, followed by fruit and ice-cream, he announced that he was driving out to see how the harvesting of the wheat was progressing.

'Would any of you like to join me?' he asked.

To his relief, the countess said she was going to have a rest before the evening's entertainment, and neither Tassya nor Sophia showed enthusiasm for a drive in the open carriage under the blazing sun.

'Perhaps Valerie would like to see how the wheat is gathered?' said Andrei, guessing at Pyotr's intention.

'She always stays with me,' said the countess, as Conrad arrived to help her upstairs.

'I don't suppose Valerie has managed to leave the house at all since being with you, countess,' said Andrei, with a gentle smile. 'This is supposed to be the day when we thank her for her kindness to you, as well as spoiling the birthday girl,' he added swiftly,

250

noticing Tassya's frown.

'I'm sure Valerie won't want to drive out at this hour of the day,' said Sophia.

'But I should like to go,' said Valerie. It would be her only chance to see Pyotr, and a short time away from Countess Irina would be bliss.

'That's settled then,' said Pyotr.

On hearing that Andrei was going with them, Sophia relaxed, and once the three ladies had departed for their various chambers Valerie followed the men out into the hallway. She was watching Pyotr giving orders to Feodor when Andrei attracted her attention.

'If you will excuse me, Miss Marsh,' he said formally, bowing before her, 'I think a short nap out on the verandah is what I desire most at present.' As he lifted his head she saw his eyes were glinting with amusement. 'Will you forgive me if I do not join you in your drive through the wheat fields?'

'I understand completely, Andrei Odarka,' she said, with a gracious inclination of her head. But her heart was singing.

Valerie didn't know how much Pyotr had told his friend about their plans for the future, but Andrei was obviously aware of their difficulties and was giving them a longed-for opportunity to be alone together.

When Pyotr came to join them, Andrei explained that he would not be accompanying them, and Pyotr burst out laughing and clapped him on the shoulder.

'You are a friend, indeed, Odarka, and one day you must allow me to repay this debt.'

'Do not stay away too long,' said Andrei. 'Remember that this is Tassya's birthday and I do not want it ruined by some thoughtless behaviour by her brother.'

'We will be back in plenty of time to dress for the special occasion, I promise you that,' said Pyotr. 'Come, Valerie, I want you to see one of the most beautiful and satisfying sights on Mavara.'

As Feodor opened the front door for them, Valerie gasped as the hot dusty air of the courtyard engulfed her.

'It will be better once we are moving,' said Pyotr, taking her lightly by the arm and leading her down the steps towards the waiting carriage that had been brought round for them. 'Feodor gave me this for you,' he said, handing her a neatly folded scarlet kerchief. 'He says you are not to go out bareheaded, Valerie Marsh, and has obviously realized you do not possess a summer hat.'

'How thoughtful of him,' she said, surprised by the unexpected kindness. She unfolded the scarf and placed it over her head, low on the forehead, then tied it at the nape of her white neck. Some of the maids wore their kerchiefs tied beneath their chins but in that intense heat Valerie wanted nothing around her throat. 'What about you?' she said.

'I wear my hat enough on duty,' said Pyotr, 'so now it is a pleasure to feel the air on my head. You look like a little peasant girl. That is not meant impolitely,' he said quickly, 'just nice and pretty and young, Varinka.'

The scarlet gave colour to her drab grey cotton and with her happiness as well as the sunshine, her cheeks were glowing.

'I am glad my appearance pleases you. Let's make the most of these precious moments, Pyotr. I am so looking forward to this drive with you.'

It had been such a long time since she had been free to go out of doors and see the countryside. She wished she and Pyotr could simply take off and disappear into the distance leaving the house, and its three annoying females, behind. Unfortunately those three were part of Pyotr Silakov's life and, if she loved him, she would always have to accept their claim on him.

After helping Valerie up into the carriage, Pyotr took the reins and they moved briskly out of the courtyard through the big iron gates and on to a rough track over the fields.

As he glanced down at her sitting small and erect beside him with her scarlet headscarf, he longed to draw up the horses and take her in his arms. But he had promised Andrei they would not be late back, and there would be time for kisses in the near future.

'We will find our love-nest, Varinka,' he said, 'and I will make sure you are comfortably settled there before I depart for Tsarskoe Selo.'

'But what about your mother?' she said, not quite believing what he said. 'I can't just walk out on her.'

'Mother will be cared for, do not worry. I shall speak to Feodor and if he says more servants are needed then we will *have* more servants. I'll not allow anyone in my family to suffer and Mother must have all the care and attention she craves. But not from you, my love.'

Pyotr's eyes were tender as he gazed down at her.

'You have done enough for my womenfolk — have worked harder than any servant — and now you will receive your reward. You'll have a home of your own, servants to care for you, and a man who loves you very much even if he is not always there to tell so.'

'That will be wonderful,' said Valerie,

turning her head and nuzzling against his lightly clad arm. 'And I, in turn, promise never to intrude upon your marriage. But I shall be waiting for you always.'

She did not know how this could all be arranged — there was so little time before he had to return to his duties — but her trust in him was complete.

Pyotr put out a hand to hold her fiercely against him for a moment then, as they approached the harvesters, he let her go and stared grimly ahead.

Dear God, help me to keep all my women happy, he prayed.

He did not intend going into marriage in a light-hearted, fickle way. He meant to make Sophia a good husband and wanted her to be content with him and her new home. He also wanted his mother and sister to be happy in the coming years. But most of all he wanted his Little England to feel safe, and needed, and adored.

'Here we are,' he said, driving the horses off the track and onto the field, where the stacks of sheaves were rising as high as the peasants' own cottages.

Valerie was surprised to see so many women at work, but Pyotr explained that the men were employed at the beet factory on the other side of the estate.

With backs bent, sharp scythes swinging in their hands, the women were bending and slashing and stacking in an easy rhythmical motion, appearing unaffected by the heat and dusty chaff-filled air.

Children of all ages were helping their mothers sometimes two or three together, staggering over the stubble with their sheaf.

As they rode slowly between the rows, Valerie saw one woman sitting with her back to a stack, feeding her newborn baby. And further on was another baby sleeping peacefully in a little tent that had been made of rags tied to three posts that protected it from the sun.

How she would love a child.

'You are very quiet,' said Pyotr, on the homeward journey, after he had spoken to one of the older women and agreed to them taking every third sheaf for themselves. 'Is the heat bothering you, Varinka?'

'No,' she said, staring ahead with troubled eyes. 'I was thinking of our unborn children and wondering what sort of a life they would have, as illegitimate offspring of our illicit union.'

'Valerie, don't use such words!' Pyotr drew on the reins and stopped the horses before turning and reaching out for her. 'They will be our love children, my darling!' He held her hard against his chest. 'I shall love them as much as any I may have with Sophia. Don't you understand, my heart?' Moving back a little he placed a hand beneath her chin and lifted her rosy, scarlet-framed face to his. 'Our children will be special as our love is special,' he said.

Then, regardless of time, he kissed her as he had wanted to kiss her since arriving at Mavara.

Valerie melted in his arms, putting her hands behind his head and pressing her thin body against his, feeling his masculine strength with renewed joy.

With one swift action, Pyotr lifted his hand to remove her kerchief and with it went most of her pins, allowing her hair to fall in rumpled abandon onto her narrow shoulders.

'My beauty, my lovely one, my heart's ease,' he muttered, burying his face in her soft curls, then running his lips down her small straight nose before covering her open, breathless mouth once more.

'Pyotr — stop!' She pulled away, shaking her head so that the curls swung backwards and forwards across her flushed face. 'We must get back. It is getting late. Oh, heavens, what shall I do with my hair?'

She had visions of Sophia's furious face, Tassya's malicious gaze, the countess's frown, as she appeared with Pyotr in the carriage with her head uncovered, her hair in disarray, and her mouth bruised from his kisses.

Carefully she began fumbling along the seat searching for her lost pins.

'Cover your hair with the kerchief, Varinka, and it will do quite well until you get to your room. I do not understand why women pay such attention to elaborate and tricky hairstyles,' he went on, calling to the horses and giving the reins a flick, 'when their wonderful hair is one of the most beautiful things about them. Like yours is now, Varinka.'

Pyotr glanced down as she continued to tut and search and fumble with her unruly locks.

'Every female I have known has spent hours at her dressing-table with her maid pulling and pinning and tweaking and coiling, until all the glory has vanished into what looks like a loaf of bread!'

In an instant Valerie's happiness disappeared and she sat upright, clutching at her scarlet kerchief with hot, sticky hands. Every female he had known. Those words had been spoken with the confidence of a man who had seen many women in their bedrooms busy at their toilette, and her heart fell like a stone to the soles of her worn, scuffed shoes.

How many women had Pyotr Silakov

known? To how many had he vowed undying love, as he now vowed to Valerie and had doubtless promised his approaching bride?

This handsome, charming, lovable man had promised her and her unborn children all the love in the world, and she believed him. But how many others had received such vows before her? And how many more would hear such words once he was married, and had settled his doting little mistress in some secluded apartment?

The idea of children also worried her despite Pyotr's reassuring words. If she thought the matter out sensibly, away from his seductive caresses and passionate kisses, how could she give her children a normal life with a father who came only infrequently to see them?

There would be no family to shelter them; they could never visit Mavara to meet their aunt or grandmother, or any half-brothers or half-sisters they might have; nor could they ever be taken to England and introduced to their grandfather in Putney.

She, Valerie Marsh, alone and unwed, would have to bear the brunt of all their questions as they grew older, the mockery of their friends, the scorn and possible rejection of their friends' parents. She would love them most dearly and knew that Pyotr would love them whenever he was with them. But did she have the strength to cope most of the time on her own?

Slowly she tied the crumpled scarf around her head, hiding the loose flowing locks that Pyotr found so entrancing, and which demonstrated her immoral ways to the world.

'There — you look prim and proper once again, Varinka,' said Pyotr's confident, amused voice beside her. When she didn't reply he glanced down in surprise. 'Why such a strange expression? There is nobody here to see you, my love, and we are back in time to prepare for our picnic by the lake. Smile and look happy, Little England.'

Still she did not smile and before he could question her further they were entering the wide iron gates and driving into the courtyard. Feodor flung open the front door and stood waiting to greet them, and a stable lad ran forward to take the reins.

Pyotr leapt down from his seat and walked round to assist Valerie onto the cobbled yard, wondering what had changed his laughing tousled Varinka into this tight-lipped crone?

With a quick nod she walked away from him towards the open doorway. There was no chance of more discussion then and unlikely to be any for the rest of that day. What the devil was she playing at?

Cursing the lack of time left for them, and the impossibility of any private talk, Pyotr watched the small grey figure with the scarlet headscarf climb the stairs, before he followed more purposefully and went into the study.

He needed a drink before going upstairs. He was in a foul mood and Valerie's extraordinary behaviour had ruined his anticipation of the approaching party.

Pyotr had always prided himself on his understanding of women. He had known enough, heaven knew, and should have been able to cope with anything this infuriating little foreigner did. Yet time after time his Varinka had both surprised and confused him, and now she had placed him in another quandary. Was this petulant behaviour contrived to make him show more interest in her? Was she hoping to make him marry her despite the impossibility of such a match?

Grabbing the bottle of vodka, Pyotr poured himself a generous amount before lifting the glass and swallowing the contents.

That was better.

He knew Valerie loved him, just as he loved her, so it was up to him to take charge of the situation and organize their future together.

17

Later that afternoon Valerie put all worries behind her for a few hours. It would be foolish to wander around with a miserable face when it would do neither her, nor her present circumstances, any good. She would try to forget about the future and concentrate instead on the cray-fishing and Tassya's surprise.

By five o'clock the sun was lower in the sky and beginning to lose its fierce heat, so a small train of carriages and carts began queuing up in the courtyard. A pony and trap were there for the countess and Valerie, and two drozhkys for Pyotr and Sophia, Tassya and Andrei. The carts were there to transport all the provisions and utensils as well as Sidor Novatko, Conrad, Feodor, Dunya, and Sophia's maid, Vera.

Wishing yet again that she had something special to wear for the celebrations, Valerie put on her newly washed and very faded blue cotton dress, and tied back her carefully brushed hair with a blue velvet ribbon grudgingly given to her by the countess.

It was Tassya's evening, and Valerie had

spent her few precious hours with Pyotr, so would now concentrate on his sister. Tassya still refused to have anything to do with her, but if she had regained the use of her legs maybe, in the excitement of recovery and in Valerie's very genuine pleasure, then maybe she and Tassya could be friends again. At least for the time she remained living at Mavara.

At 5.20 Conrad came up to collect the countess and Valerie followed them down the stairs to where the young men, and Tassya in her chair, were waiting.

'I suppose Sophia is going to make a grand entrance,' said Pyotr sarcastically, irritated by his betrothed's tardiness and still smarting from Valerie's hasty retreat after their happy time together. But he felt better when she flashed him a quick smile before following Conrad and the countess out into the yard.

Thank heavens, she was his loving Little England once again.

As Valerie climbed into the little trap and took her place beside the countess, she glanced back to see Pyotr appearing in the doorway with Sophia on his arm. Then she gave a gasp of admiration at the vision on the top step.

Countess Irina also looked back as she gathered up the reins.

'Quite unsuitable for a picnic!' she snapped.

But Valerie remained silent, her eyes wide in astonishment.

Sophia was clad in a dress of brilliant green silk, low cut and sleeveless, gathered tightly at her knees by an enormous green brooch encrusted with silver, and then trailing to her ankles.

'She can scarcely walk,' said the countess. 'And look at her shoes!'

Sophia teetered on the highest pair of black satin shoes Valerie had ever seen, which were decorated with the same green and silver stones. Over her tight-fitting dress was a delicately pleated tunic of green silk edged with black braid, and a cummerbund of black satin encased her slender waist.

'I believe it is called a hobble-skirt,' said Valerie, finding her voice at last.

She remembered how she and Grand Duchess Olga had studied a French fashion magazine called 'La Gazette du Bon Ton' and how they had become quite hysterical laughing at some of the more outrageous fashion plates.

Quickly Valerie put such memories out of her mind. It wouldn't do to think about those happy days with the Imperial family. So she concentrated on Sophia Lukaev instead.

The beauty from St Petersburg certainly

possessed the audacity and the figure to wear such daring attire and look splendid in it. A tiny green cap was perched on top of her built-up hair, and at the back of her head two ostrich feathers swooped, dyed black to match the braiding on her tunic and the satin at her waist.

Valerie wondered what Pyotr thought about such an extravaganza, but his face was expressionless as he helped Sophia down the steps. When they reached their carriage he had to pick her up in his arms and place her carefully into the drozhky. There was no way she could have climbed into it herself.

'Off we go!' shouted the countess. 'We have wasted enough time on that young lady and I want my food.'

She gave the reins a flick and they began to move slowly away from the house and down the slope towards the lake. Once it was reached, Countess Irina was helped to the water's edge by Conrad and given a folding stool to sit on. Then he produced a stick with a line on the end of it, and tied on a small lump of meat.

'This is how cray-fishing is done at Mavara,' she said, dangling her line into the water. 'You hold the net, Valerie, and if I catch something get that net under it *at once*, you hear?'

Valerie nodded, taking the long-handled

net from Conrad, who then returned to the cart and began collecting more lines and nets and folding stools for the others.

Behind them, Sidor Novatko was building a fire on which he placed two bricks, then a heavy pot filled with water. Vera and Dunya were throwing raw potatoes onto the flames and Feodor was busy with a white cloth. He spread it out on the grass then placed plates and bowls of salad, and glasses and bottles of wine upon it.

Tassya sat in her chair close to the water's edge where Andrei assisted her with rod and line, and Pyotr leaned lazily against the side of the open carriage, chatting to Sophia in her green and black elegance.

'I suppose she will remain perched up there for the entire evening,' said the countess. 'I knew that was a stupid garment to wear. She won't be able to join in our picnic at all.'

'Pyotr will look after her,' said Valerie, thinking how pleasant it would be to be dressed in one's best, seated high above everyone else, and to be served food and wine by an attentive lover.

Hastily she looked across at Tassya, who was talking to Andrei. When would she surprise them? Presumably when the food was cooked and the first glasses raised to congratulate her?

Suddenly there was a shriek from the countess and dangling on the end of her line was a very large crayfish.

'Quickly, Valerie — the net, the net!'

Grabbing hold of her net, Valerie swung it beneath the creature and managed to capture it before it could fall back into the water.

'We are the first,' said Countess Irina, with satisfaction. 'I may be old and useless in many ways but I can still catch crayfish. Take it over to Sidor, Valerie, I'm getting hungry.'

Valerie hurried with her struggling burden over to the roaring fire, where Sidor plunged it into the boiling pot.

As nobody else proved successful after that, Tassya became impatient.

'Go on, Dunya,' she said. 'Jump into the water and catch some for us. We need more than one.' She grinned at Valerie as the maid obediently walked a little way down the bank and began removing her clothes. 'Don't you wish you could join her, Valerie Marsh?'

'No, thank you,' said Valerie, turning her head away as the pink, well-rounded form of Dunya began walking sedately into the lake.

'We were only joking,' said the countess beside her, 'but it is a good way of catching these darned creatures.'

Valerie realized that the countess was enjoying herself. All her ailments were forgotten and she was out in the fresh air, behaving like a normal human being once more. I'll suggest a drive around the estate tomorrow, thought Valerie. It will do us both good after being shut away in those rooms upstairs. I will see and learn more about Mavara, and the countess will be encouraged to take an interest in things again.

Just as she was pondering there came a shout from across the water and everyone stared in surprise at the far bank. Silhouetted against the red sky was a black figure on horseback, gesticulating into the air.

'Who the devil is that?' asked Pyotr, moving away from the carriage and raising his hand to his eyes as he gazed at the unexpected stranger.

The man was yelling so hoarsely and so quickly that Valerie couldn't understand him, but Pyotr heard and so did Andrei.

With a muffled exclamation, Andrei left Tassya's side and went to join his friend.

'We hear you, Lev Garbuz,' shouted Pyotr. 'Tell them we are coming!'

'What was that about?' said the countess, whilst Sophia called plaintively from her seat in the carriage.

Valerie, staring at Pyotr as he came striding back towards them, saw excitement blazing in his eyes.

'That was Lev Garbuz from Kamenka. He has received a telegraph from St Petersburg. Germany has declared war and we must return to Tsarskoe Selo at once.'

'Oh no.' The countess's voice was scarcely above a whisper.

Pyotr nodded then leaned forward to grasp one of her hands.

'The Tsar is issuing a formal proclamation of hostilities tomorrow,' he said, 'that Germany is in a state of war with Holy Russia.'

Despite the gravity of such unexpected news, he was elated. There would be no marriage to Sophia for the time being, and he could get away to face the enemy with a good horse under him, and a lethal sabre gleaming in his hand.

Andrei, too, felt an enormous sense of relief. He, more than Pyotr, had feared the future because of the growing unrest amongst the peasants. Now war would unite them all. It would be a joining of noble and commoner, prince and peasant, in the battle to protect Holy Russia. And all thought of revolution would be erased.

★ ★ ★

Quickly, Pyotr and Andrei bade farewell to the women. After kissing his mother, Pyotr

269

turned to Valerie and held her hands tightly in his.

'Stay here,' he said. 'Stay at Mavara and I will be in touch.' Then he walked away to hug his weeping sister.

'You can't go yet!' cried Tassya. 'It's my birthday and you haven't seen my surprise.'

'Keep it, Tassya — another time.' Pyotr left her and hurried over to the drozhky where he reached for Sophia's hand and held it briefly to his lips. 'Hurry, Odarka,' he called over his shoulder. 'A train leaves Kamenka at 9.30 and we'll catch it if we are quick.'

Andrei bent over Tassya's trembling form.

'Your surprise will last,' he said. 'We will get leave once all this has been sorted out and we'll be down again for a proper celebration then. Just be patient, Tassya.'

Then he ran for the second drozhky after a hurried bow towards the countess and Valerie.

'What about me?' wailed Sophia, sitting green and beautiful in her carriage as the men disappeared down the track in a cloud of dust.

They intended picking up a few belongings from the house before leaving for Kamenka and a train north to the capital.

For those remaining behind there was a terrible feeling of anticlimax. Countess Irina sat staring ahead of her over the water, her rod dangling limply in her hands. Tassya continued to sob quietly and Sophia's wailing dwindled to a depressed silence.

The servants huddled around the fire uncertain whether food was to be eaten, or not. And further along the bank Dunya began to dry herself and put on her clothing, having caught nothing.

Sighing, Valerie walked back to the fire.

'Open the wine, Feodor,' she said, 'and get the plates ready for the potatoes and salad. Divide up the crayfish and we'll eat and drink before going back.'

Feodor nodded, grateful for orders, and immediately the little group around the fire became busy, preparing for the repast.

Ignoring Sophia, Valerie went across to stand beside Tassya.

'What is your surprise?' she said clearly.

Tassya shrugged, her face lowered in misery.

'What's the use?' she said. 'Nothing matters now.'

'Of course it matters! Now, more than ever before — everything matters, Tassya! Your country is at war and will need every man, woman, and child, to give it support and show courage and hope for the future. Tell me, have you regained the use of your legs?'

Tassya flashed the English girl a look of disdain.

'Yes, Valerie Marsh, I can walk again thanks to the prayers of Father Grigorii. But what use is that when nobody can see me?'

'For goodness sake, pull yourself together!' Valerie could have slapped the tear-streaked woeful face. 'You have been healed and that is the most wonderful thing that could ever have happened to you: Get up, Tassya,' she shouted. 'Go and show your mother what you can do. Now!'

Valerie's voice was so loud that Tassya sniffed and obeyed. Without difficulty, moving with new-found agility, she stood up then walked slowly across the grass to her mother.

'I can walk again, Mother,' she said, bending over the silent woman, whose head jerked up before she gave a cry and lifted her arms to embrace her daughter.

With a smile Valerie watched the pair, then she turned and gave the wheelchair a shove over the bank where it sank slowly into the water. Tassya heard the splash and straightened, staring at the place where her chair had stood.

'My chair!' she cried, pulling away from the countess and moving towards Valerie. 'How dare you throw it in the water!'

'You won't be needing it again,' said Valerie. 'You can walk now and it's time you led a normal life at Mavara. Your mother needs you, the estate needs you, and whilst Pyotr is away it'll be up to you to keep things running smoothly. Thank God you are now fit enough to take on such a challenge.'

A challenge? Tassya liked the sound of that and the thought of responsibility at last. Maybe she could do it, and prove to both Pyotr and Andrei how capable she was.

'Will somebody please pay attention to me?' Sophia's voice floated across to them.

Hastily Vera ran forward to collect a plate from Feodor and Valerie did the same, realizing that none of them had eaten for hours and sustenance was needed before they could plan for the future. She hoped the men had been able to grab something from the kitchen before departing.

After helping the countess move nearer her future daughter-in-law and settling her on the folding stool with a plate of food and glass of wine, Valerie collected some more for herself before sitting down next to Tassya on the grass.

At first all the talk was centred on the young girl and her miraculous recovery, and Valerie listened to praise for Grigorii Rasputin without interrupting. This was

Tassya's day and although the men were not there to enjoy her revelation, it was important for her to receive attention and congratulations from her mother and Sophia.

Whatever Valerie thought of the man from Siberia, there was no doubt that he could work miracles.

Once their hunger had been assuaged, thoughts turned once more to the news from St Petersburg.

'What will you do now, Sophia?' asked Valerie.

It was surprisingly easy to talk to her. With the men gone they were all in the same situation. Women with no husbands, or lovers, or brothers, to lead them.

'I shall return to St Petersburg tomorrow with Vera,' said Sophia. 'I must know where Pyotr is being sent and will find out all the details in the capital.'

'Write to me,' said the countess. 'Pyotr may not have the time and I wish to know everything. Write and tell me what is happening to our beloved Russia. And remind Conrad to take a boy with him to the station so he can bring back the other carriage,' she told Valerie.

Valerie nodded, then they all sat in silent thought, wondering when they would see the men they loved again.

18

The following days passed slowly and the three women at Mavara lived as if in a vacuum, uncertain what to do with their lives. Once Sophia had departed, time seemed to stand still as they waited for news from the outside world.

Valerie wrote to Grand Duchess Olga, hoping that now such a colossal event had occurred the past drama with Rasputin could be forgotten by Olga, and she would be able to reply in her old friendly style.

Certainly Tassya's enmity had disappeared since the devastating news of war, and she was seeking Valerie's company once more.

'Sorry I was so nasty to you,' she said, coming up to join Valerie one afternoon whilst Countess Irina had her nap in the adjoining bedroom. 'Can we forget all about that, please, and be friends again?'

'I would like nothing better,' said Valerie, lifting her head from the grey dress she was patching, and smiling. 'I will never like Grigorii Rasputin, but he has to be praised for what he has done for you. Sit down and rest your legs — they mustn't be overworked in your excitement.'

Tassya grinned, flinging herself into the big apricot armchair opposite her companion.

'They do get weary, but I wake up every morning with joy in my heart, knowing I can get out of bed and go anywhere I like without calling for Dunya.' Her face sobered. 'I just wish Pyotr and Andrei could have seen me walking.'

'They will come down on leave and that is why you must learn all you can from your mother, Tassya. Learn about the estate and see that it remains in good order for when Pyotr comes home.'

Tassya nodded. 'I'll do that. It will keep me busy whilst we wait.'

Valerie also managed to keep occupied, attending to the countess's every need, but she was not content and longed for something to fill her mind until she saw Pyotr again.

Their plans for the future had been hopelessly disrupted by the war and she didn't know where to go, or what to do. Pyotr had said stay at Mavara until he contacted her. But it might be weeks, months even, before she heard from him and she couldn't make Mavara her home because of Sophia.

And what about the betrothed couple? Would Pyotr get leave in time for the wedding? Would they come down to Mavara in September as man and wife? Would Sophia then stay on as mistress of the estate?

All she had to remind her of Pyotr was a small knotted kerchief, the scarlet one she had worn on their ride through the wheatfields, and which she had found in her bedroom when returning from the picnic. Inside was a scrap of paper wrapped around ten roubles, on which was written: 'Use this to buy yourself a new dress'.

Valerie put the money away in her empty purse. She had no intention of buying anything at present. But the little note with Pyotr's strong, downward-stroked handwriting, was folded and slipped into her bodice close to her heart.

The first letter to arrive at Mavara was for Valerie. It was from Grand Duchess Olga, and was as warm and friendly as Valerie had hoped.

' . . . We are all well and very busy at Catherine Palace, which has been converted into a military hospital,' she wrote. 'Mother is in her element organizing a nursing course for me and Tatiana and Anna Vyrubova, and soon we will be assisting in the wards. Dear Valerie, I do wish you were here but if you can ever get to Kiev try and work in a hospital there.

'I fear that casualties will be heavy as the war progresses, and nursing is something we can do well. It is also a splendid way of helping our brave men . . . '

Olga also informed Valerie that her father, in a burst of patriotic enthusiasm, had changed the name of his capital to the Slav word — Petrograd.

So it was St Petersburg no longer. Yet another change in this ever-changing world. Valerie was grateful for Olga's news and suddenly confident about her own future. At last she knew what she was going to do.

Nurses would be needed more and more as the weeks went by. Her knowledge of Russian was good enough for her to understand most of what was said even if her speech was not perfect. And if, God forbid, Pyotr were ever wounded and sent home to recuperate, she would know exactly how to care for him.

Fortunately she had the money he had left her. She would ask Conrad to drive her to Kamenka and she would take the first train to Kiev. Then she would offer her assistance at the first hospital she found there.

Valerie knew her decision would not please the countess, but Tassya was quite capable of running the household with Feodor, and Galina could assist the countess.

Valerie was quite determined and a great

weight had lifted from her chest. She would get away from Mavara at last and had the money to pay for her escape.

Getting away was far from easy, however, as both the countess and her daughter became angrier and angrier on seeing that Valerie meant every word she said.

'Quite ridiculous!' snapped Countess Irina, knowing that her life would become desolate without the company of the English girl.

She would be cared for by Galina, or Masha, or whoever else she demanded to help her. But none of the peasants possessed Valerie's quiet intelligence; none would laugh at her dry comments, nor show the sympathy that Valerie portrayed.

'How can you possibly nurse when you are a girl of decent upbringing and breeding? Have you any idea of the injuries of war? Have you any notion of the appalling stench, and the sight of mangled, screaming young bodies begging to die?'

Valerie was not going to be put off by unpleasant thoughts. Besides, her upbringing and breeding had not been considered at Mavara when she had carried endless trays up and down the stairs, washed and dressed the grumbling countess, and been frequently disturbed at night. In a way, she had been trained in advance for what was to come.

Apart from the injuries.

'I shall learn how to cope,' she said.

'Well, I think you are mean!' said Tassya. 'Leaving us in the lurch and going off to do what you want. What about us here? What about Mother and me? And I heard Pyotr telling you to stay at Mavara,' she ended defiantly.

'I am thinking of Pyotr,' said Valerie, 'and of Andrei Odarka. If either of them should be wounded and sent back here to convalesce, would you know how to care for their wounds?'

'No, but we have servants enough to help. We could manage.'

'Well, I intend learning all I can and nothing you say will prevent me from going. But I will send you my address the moment I have found accommodation and I promise you — ' she looked at her companions with steady eyes — 'if Pyotr or Andrei should be returned here injured, I will give up my work at the hospital and come back to nurse them. Does that satisfy you?'

The countess remained silent, but Tassya nodded, and the following week Conrad drove Valerie to Kamenka where she caught the train to Kiev and her new life.

* * *

In a large square off the Kreschatik — the Street of the Cross Valerie was accepted at once as a nursing student in the hospital.

And at the end of August came news of a massive Russian defeat at the Battle of Tannenberg, which made her thankful she had made the move when she had.

'Fortunately for us it is on the Northern Front,' said the harassed Nurse-in-Charge, 'so we should not have to take in too many extra casualties.'

She did not have nearly enough nurses, nor beds, but as the southern armies were holding their own against the Austrians, all the wounded being transferred back to her hospital in Kiev were adequately cared for at present.

'Pray for continual victories in the south,' she told her nurses with a grim smile, 'and we will be able to cope.'

★　★　★

Every night Valerie wondered where Pyotr had been sent. She had received no news of him, although Tassya had promised to write. She prayed that he was fighting the Austrians and had not been sent to the Northern Front, where the real battle-grounds lay against the vastly efficient German armies.

She had been fortunate in finding a room in a house but five minutes walk from the hospital. In her white uniform with the red cross on the sleeve and the nun-like headdress that fell to her shoulders, she felt capable and proficient.

Valerie liked the other girls who were nursing students with her, and respected the large, severe-faced Nurse-in-Charge. But her feet in their sturdy black leather shoes ached from endless standing on the hard, cold floors of the ward, and her heart ached for the pain and misery she saw daily.

What conditions were like in the north she dared not contemplate, for the Battle of Tannenberg was said to have cost Russia 100,000 men. Here in the south, despite glorious victories over the Austrians in Galicia, there were still fearful injuries.

Every day hundreds of wounded and dying men were brought into Kiev by Red Cross trains.

'Keep smiling,' said the Nurse-in-Charge. 'The men must never see you upset, or worried, about their condition.'

Valerie often remembered Countess Irina's words of gloom as she washed torn flesh and tried to bandage what was left of it, whilst still looking cheerful. Even worse than the war injuries were the amputations, which took place daily in the operating room.

Rotten fingers were removed stinking of poisoned blood, as were entire arms and legs. Terrible, shattering wounds in the groin were unbearable to look at, but had to be washed and cleaned, painted with iodine and smeared with Vaseline, before being covered over as gently as possible.

Dear God, don't let this happen to Pyotr, she prayed, remembering his fine masculine body brimming with good health and beauty. For these young men had also been fit and splendid once, until war robbed them of their splendour, some even of their manhood.

Then one day came the news she had feared.

19

Kiev

'Hey, nurse, you come from somewhere near Kamenka, don't you?'

The Nurse-in-Charge came striding down the long corridor that led to the stairs and halted in front of the weary English girl.

Valerie nodded, wondering what was to follow. She was about to leave the hospital and return to her room for a few hours of desperately needed sleep.

'Then go into the lower ward and see if you can get any sense out of the patient by the door. We can get nothing from him and all his papers have been destroyed. One of the nurses thought she heard him mentioning Kamenka when he was delirious. He is awake now, but remains silent. Go and see if you can find out who he is, Valerie Marsh.'

Could it be Pyotr? Valerie's heart began to thud.

'Is he badly injured?'

'Not nearly as bad as some, but he doesn't seem to *want* to recover. Go and see what you can do. If he is determined to die we can use his bed.'

The Nurse-in-Charge had no time for awkward patients when so many were desperate for attention, and grateful for what the nurses were doing for them. The little foreigner had a way with her, a gentleness that seemed to calm and comfort even the most distressed of the wounded soldiers. Maybe she could sort out the difficult newcomer.

Valerie hurried down the stairs and flung open the door to the lower ward, her fatigue forgotten. To her right was a body so completely bandaged she couldn't see his face. But on the other side, sitting up against his pillows and staring ahead of him, was Pyotr.

His left hand and arm were bandaged, as was his head so his hair was not visible. But beneath the strips that half-covered his face, his right eye blazed out in bitter anger above his strong nose and tightly clamped lips. She had recognized that profile at once.

Slowly Valerie walked to the bed and looked down at him.

'Hello, Pyotr,' she said.

He glanced up and then away again, without a smile. But he knew her.

'What are you doing here?' he said.

'I came to Kiev to be trained as a nursing sister. I wanted to help all the brave men in this terrible war. Oh, Petya, it is so good to see you again.' She couldn't put her arms around him for fear of hurting him, but she fell to her knees and gently touched his good hand. 'Thank God you are safe. I have worried so much about you. Are you in pain? What happened to you?'

She gazed at the man she loved wanting to kiss his hard-pressed lips and stroke his lean cheek. His skin was still tanned despite his wounds and appeared very brown beneath the white bandages. But there was nothing welcoming about his hostile position.

'Go away,' he said. 'I don't wish to talk.'

He turned his head away from her loving face and looked across at the endless row of beds all filled with broken, immobile bodies.

God! How he wished he were dead.

He had tried so hard to save his friend. He had seen Andrei fall from his horse a few yards away and had dismounted, intending to run to him. But in that instant a shell had exploded throwing him to one side and opening up a crater large enough to bury a house.

Shell splinters had pierced his left side and he had been unconscious for days. But once they had operated to remove the fragments, he had regained enough of his senses to ask about Andrei.

His friend had vanished along with twenty others, he was informed. Then he, Count Pyotr Silakov, was transferred to Kiev.

In a very short period of time at the front, Pyotr had realized that cavalry was of little use in modern warfare. The Russian cavalry, with its shining sabres and pounding horses, was totally helpless against the machine guns of the enemy.

Their bravery was never in doubt, but the reckless gallantry of the charge was quickly demolished when superior artillery scythed down the Russian ranks like rows of wheat.

As Andrei Odarka had said, aeons ago it seemed now, Russia possessed the men, but was sadly lacking in rifles, munitions, and artillery. And, thought Pyotr bitterly, because of the enormous size of his beloved land, lack of sufficient railways made it impossible to transport supplies to where they were most needed.

To make matters worse, he had lost his best friend and been sent away from the front to recover in a hospital ward.

What use would he be to anyone with a mutilated arm and disfigured face? Pyotr's head ached abominably and he couldn't bear Valerie Marsh seeing him like this. What the hell was she doing trotting around in that stiff white uniform and those ugly boots?

The other nurses irritated him with their bossy ways and quick capable hands, but Valerie was not going to touch him. He had always been the strong one in the past, the demanding lover with searching fingers and caressing lips. He was not going to lie there, hideous and helpless, whilst she prodded and poked him.

Pyotr wanted to be left alone to sink ever deeper into misery and hatred of the entire world.

'Nurse!' he shouted, raising his head and yelling across the quiet ward. 'I want the Nurse-in-Charge to get this foreign girl away from me!'

At first Valerie was worried by the change in Pyotr. This was a stranger and not the man she had once adored. Had the head wound affected his sanity?

But as she watched his tense, furious face and heard the strength in his voice, she suspected that he was not as badly hurt as she had feared and that his pride was probably the most wounded part of him.

Remembering the handsome and confident young officer with whom she had fallen in love, Valerie knew his injuries must be depressing him. But Pyotr had to understand how fortunate he was.

She thought of the young man who had died in her arms that very morning, and of the two who would surely die that night, or next day. Two young lads who lay uncomplaining, thankful for her comforting words as they waited for death in unrelieved agony.

Grimly she dragged her weary body to its feet.

'I will not come again, Count Pyotr Silakov,' she said loudly, causing him to turn his head in surprise at the sound of her voice. 'Go on, yell as much as you like though I doubt if anyone will come. We are all too busy caring for the ones who really need us, and who are grateful for the hours we spend trying to help them. You should be glad you still have a life ahead of you. I will make sure your family is informed of your whereabouts.'

Then she turned on her sturdy black heel and marched out of the ward.

20

Tassya was the first to visit Pyotr after Valerie. She telegraphed the time and day of her arrival and came to the hospital with Dunya, asking for Valerie Marsh.

'I wanted to see you before him,' she said, as they stood in the passage outside Valerie's ward. 'How badly hurt is he?'

Tassya looked exhausted. Travelling was difficult now that so many troops were being sent to the front, and railway carriages, cattle trucks, and goods trains, were all being used bringing the wounded back to hospitals in the Ukraine.

Fortunately, Pyotr's hospital was the one nearest to the railway station.

'Is he in terrible pain?' asked Tassya. 'Will I be able to see him without weeping?' Her face was pale beneath her wolf-skin hat and Dunya was carrying a walking-stick although Tassya had not used it. 'Will he be able to come home soon?'

Valerie reached out to pat the girl's fur-clad arm.

'You will have to ask the Nurse-in-Charge,' she said. 'I am occupied on this second floor and haven't seen Pyotr since sending you news of him. I don't think he is in much pain and hope he can soon be sent back to Mavara. He is proving a difficult patient.'

Tassya nodded. 'He was never good at sitting still and doing nothing. And we want him home, Valerie. So many of our men have been called up, Mother and I are not coping very well on our own. Conrad left on Saturday.'

'Then tell Pyotr that,' said Valerie. 'It will be good for him to feel needed.'

'Will you come too?' said Tassya, looking at the white-clad English girl with the red cross on her sleeve.

Valerie was good with her mother, she was good at Mavara, and everything seemed more orderly when she was around.

'Andrei will be sent back shortly and we'll need your nursing skills. You did promise, Valerie.'

'I don't know,' said Valerie. So much would depend on Pyotr's wishes, and those of Sophia. 'But tell me about Andrei,' she went on quickly. 'Has he also been wounded?'

Tassya blushed. 'He sent me a very badly written letter, but he is going to be all right and will come to Mavara as soon as he's able to travel. I wrote to him as soon as you told me about Pyotr, and I also told him I was walking again.'

Valerie clapped her hands. 'Pyotr doesn't know about that! That will be excellent news for him, Tassya. I'll take you down now then I must get back to work.'

Having left Tassya and Dunya at the entrance to Pyotr's ward, she hurried upstairs again, her heart lifting with every step. If only Pyotr could be sent across to Mavara she was certain that his beloved home, and his family, would give him the courage to face life again and renew some of his old vitality.

★　★　★

As soon as his sister had left him, Pyotr went over every word of their conversation, scarcely believing what he had heard.

Tassya could walk again and Andrei was safe.

Pyotr leaned his head back against the pillows and felt his limbs relax in an enormous sense of joy and relief.

Then his thoughts returned to Valerie Marsh, and with a slight smile he remembered their first meeting at Tsarskoe Selo railway station, and how enthusiastic she had been about everything Russian, and of her growing love for the new land in which she found herself, and their own developing passion.

She was very special, his Little England, and he hadn't treated her at all well when she came to see him.

Well, he was going to do better from now on. He would be polite to the nurses, who were only doing their duty when they removed his bandages and dabbed with irritating speed at his sore head and arm.

He intended thinking positively, and would always be thankful he hadn't lost the sight of his left eye, which had at first been feared. And his head wound was healing slowly. Pyotr knew he had to accept loss of movement in his left hand, but at least his arm had not been amputated.

What worried him most was his face. The head wound would heal in time and his hair would grow back, but the left side of his face was badly scarred. He could feel the roughened weals with his fingers and knew that his good looks, as well as the chance to fight for his country, had gone forever.

Then he remembered the girl he was supposed to marry.

Oh God, he could not bear that beauty from St Petersburg seeing him in this ugly, immobile state.

Tassya had seen him, and hadn't appeared unduly shocked by his appearance, but then she knew what it was like to be helpless and dependent on others.

And Valerie Marsh, due to her daily work in the hospital, was used to injuries far worse than his and had even berated him for his self-pity.

But the last thing he wanted was for the glorious Sophia to come floating to his bedside with her furs and jewels, making shocked or sympathetic noises in her high, imperious voice.

Feverishly he prayed that she would be unable to make the long journey down to Kiev in wartime.

* * *

Two weeks later the Nurse-in-Charge informed Valerie that Count Pyotr Silakov could be discharged.

'He is demanding that you travel with him,' she said coldly. 'As there is only a young sister and an elderly mother at home, and all the men servants have been called up, there doesn't seem to be anyone else capable of travelling with him. Do you wish to accompany him, Valerie Marsh?'

'I will go,' said Valerie. She hadn't seen Pyotr since that first unpleasant encounter in the ward, but if he was asking for her now she would not refuse him. 'I will assist him on the journey and see him safely home. After that I don't know.'

So much would depend on Sophia.

'We will miss you,' said the Nurse-in-Charge. 'Come back if you can, Valerie Marsh. I fear this war is going to last a long time.'

'I will return if it is possible,' said Valerie.

Although she had been desperate to get away from Mavara, she now remembered its tranquillity after the rush and chaos of the wards, its beauty and luxury after the stench and filth of the military hospital. And here was the chance to be with Pyotr and help him rebuild his broken body and disrupted life.

He had asked for her, so that meant he wanted her near him.

★ ★ ★

The day before leaving, Valerie said goodbye to all the nursing sisters and told the Nurse-in-Charge she would come early the following morning to collect Pyotr. With train services so badly disrupted she wanted to get to the railway station as soon as possible.

Maria, the nurse who had been assisting Pyotr with his walking up and down the ward — and who did not like him very much — wished Valerie luck with the man. Count

Silakov was the most pig-headed, self-centred patient she had ever had to deal with and she was thankful not to be taking him home.

Valerie knew Pyotr so well she was sure his release would put him in a better frame of mind. Maria also told her that although Pyotr walked well without the aid of a stick, he always put unnecessary weight on her arm, which further annoyed her.

He can rest on me as much as he likes, thought Valerie, hurrying back to her room to get some sleep before morning.

The street had been shovelled free of snow for it was November already and the first snows had begun to fall. She had telegraphed Tassya to tell her when they would be leaving Kiev, and had asked for Feodor to wait at Kamenka railway station for them. They should arrive in the late afternoon, but delays were more than likely.

Valerie wasn't sure if Feodor remained at Mavara. But as he was considerably older than Conrad she hoped he had not been sent to the front. She also hoped that she would be able to get a seat for Pyotr.

Too much standing on the platform, or in the train, would not be good for his injured leg. However, she would worry about that in the morning. Now she needed to sleep.

After she had packed her few belongings

into a canvas bag she fell into bed and was instantly asleep.

But almost at once, it seemed, she was awakened by a loud rapping on her door and the voice of her landlady calling her name.

Slowly Valerie sat up, trying to gather her wits. Then she pulled on her dressing-gown and stumbled to the door.

Outside on the landing stood the owner of the house and behind her were Sophia Lukaev and her maid, Vera.

21

'I am sorry to wake you,' said Sophia, pushing past the landlady and entering the shabby room, 'but I must speak to you. Light the lamp quickly. I must get back to my hotel, but had to see you first. Thank you,' she said sharply, to the hovering woman in the doorway, 'I can let myself out.'

The landlady shrugged then disappeared down the stairs, leaving them in semi-darkness as Valerie fumbled for the matches to light the lamp.

'There,' she said, as the wick caught and she adjusted the glass shade before sitting down on the edge of the bed. Sophia perched on the only chair and Vera stood by the door. 'Have you seen Pyotr?'

Sophia looked magnificent in a sable coat and matching hat, with pearls in her ears and around her throat.

'The journey from Petrograd was unbelievably squalid,' she said. 'I had to share my compartment with three other women and it has taken over a week to get here. I cannot imagine how I'll ever get back but . . . ' she hesitated, fumbling for a tiny lace handkerchief at her wrist.

'Why have you come to me? And have you seen Pyotr?' Valerie asked again, wishing she was more prepared for this visit.

Sophia shuffled on her chair and dabbed at her mouth with the handkerchief.

'I have just come from Pyotr,' she said. 'And it was a dreadful shock, Valerie. I think he's gone mad.'

'What?' Valerie stared at her. 'Why do you say that? What did he do?'

'He didn't do, or say, anything. I don't even know whether he recognized me. I sat beside his bed. I talked to him, Valerie, but he just stared straight ahead as if I weren't there!' She began to sob. 'And his poor face — he is so disfigured — I cannot marry him, Valerie. He is not the man I once loved.'

Sophia lifted a tear-streaked face to the horrified English girl.

'He frightens and disgusts me,' she said. 'I gave him back the ring and came away. But I want you to go there, Valerie, and make sure he is all right. I'm not sure if he understood me, but I don't want to hurt him any more than he has already been hurt. And the ring, Valerie, see if that is safe.'

She dabbed at her eyes with the handkerchief as Valerie tried to take in the enormity of what she had heard.

'I shoved the ring into his good hand and came away, but I don't want it stolen, Valerie. Please go.'

Without a word Valerie slipped off her dressing-gown and began pulling on a long black skirt and thick pullover over her nightdress. Then she reached for her winter coat, which hung on a hook behind the door, and tied a scarf around her unbound hair.

'I'll go at once,' she said, buttoning up her coat. Then she glanced at the lamp and moved across to turn down the wick. 'I don't believe I shall be long, but who knows? I may have to stay longer than I intend.'

If Pyotr were in a distressed state she would have to stay with him till morning.

Then she glanced at Sophia, who was following her out of the room with Vera behind her, and felt enormous relief that this beautiful creature would soon be out of her life.

'What are you going to do now?' she asked, as they walked out onto the landing and she closed the door behind them.

'I shall return to my hotel and try to get a train to Petrograd tomorrow. The railways are in chaos so I don't know *when* I'll be home again. Thank God these are lit,' she went on, as they descended the stairs. 'What a miserable dwelling, Valerie. I don't know how you can live here.'

'I spend most of my time at the hospital,' said Valerie, following her down the sagging, uncarpeted stairs. 'But the room has served its purpose. Tomorrow I'm taking Pyotr back to Mavara.'

'Good,' said Sophia, as they reached the step into a quiet, white night where the snow fell lightly on their heads. 'Don't tell him he repulsed me. Just say I was glad to see him but am shortly to leave with my parents for America. That was the reason I broke off our engagement.'

'America?' What a long journey to make in wartime, thought Valerie.

'We'll wait until the spring and then make for Murmansk once the ice has melted. The port is in British hands and your friends, the Lees, will be returning to England that way. Mrs Lees asked me to give you her best wishes, Valerie, when I bumped into her in Alexandre's. Papa says Russia is finished, so I don't mind leaving now that I'm not going to marry Pyotr.'

At the next corner the girls went in opposite directions. As she waved goodbye to the glamorous, wealthy girl accompanied by her maid, Valerie's heart beat with unusual joy.

The Lukaev wealth was no longer available,

and Count Pyotr Silakov was no longer the dashing, handsome young officer with whom she had fallen in love. But to her neither money, nor dazzling appearances, were important. All she wanted was to love Pyotr forever. If he would let her.

Praying that Sophia had been wrong in thinking his mind had been affected, Valerie entered the hospital and made her way up to the first floor.

★ ★ ★

It was very quiet in the ward, which was lit only by a lamp at the far end where the night-sister was sitting. She glanced up on seeing Valerie, but did not call out as the girl tiptoed to Pyotr's bedside.

Mothers and wives and lovers were continually coming at any time of the day or night, so this nocturnal visit was not unusual.

For a long time Valerie gazed down at the still figure in the bed. Pyotr seemed to be sleeping peacefully and she didn't want to disturb him. Certainly there was nothing strange, or worrying, about his recumbent form.

There was no sign of the ring, however, and for Sophia's sake as well as for Countess Irina's, she felt the precious ruby and

302

platinum jewel must be found.

Cautiously she bent forward, wondering if it had slipped between the folds of the bedcovers, when Pyotr's voice made her jump.

'I didn't realize we were going to leave before the dawn.'

'You gave me a fright!' Valerie stepped back, placing a hand on her chest. 'I thought you were asleep.'

'Resting not sleeping. What do you want here, Valerie Marsh?'

She looked like a peasant woman, he thought, with the headscarf and drab winter coat. Grey, no doubt, although he couldn't make out the colour. How very different she was to the splendid scented lady, who had come to his side but a short while ago.

'Are we leaving now?' His voice was irritable, but in no way insane.

Valerie sighed. 'We are not going until morning. But Sophia has just been to see me and was very upset by . . . ' she paused . . . 'By your troubled state. She asked me to come round and make sure you were all right.'

'Troubled state? What extraordinary words to use!' Pyotr shifted up on his pillows, leaning on his good arm. 'A foolish lady, the Lukaev. I was glad to see her go,' he said.

'Pyotr! She was your future wife. Were you not upset when she returned your ring?'

His eyes glinted in the light from the distant lamp.

'I have the ring. It is the best thing I have ever received from her.'

'You are being very unkind,' said Valerie, frowning. 'Sophia and her parents are hoping to get across to America and start a new life over there. That is the reason she returned your ring. She wanted me to make sure that you were not too distressed.'

'No,' he said. 'I just didn't want her to come and see me like this, Valerie. Perhaps I treated her unkindly by ignoring her, but she means nothing to me now.' He lifted his head and stared up at the ceiling. 'Before the war Sophia was an important part of my life. But now everything has changed. Those golden days of wine and roses are gone forever.'

'Don't say that!' Valerie removed her mittens and shoved them into her pocket before reaching forward to touch Pyotr's good hand. 'The happy times will come again, and laughter and joy will return once the fighting is over.'

'Maybe, but until then I want to get back to Mavara and organize the estate. I want to make sure bread and sugar can be produced in large quantities for our troops. Tassya says most of the men have been called up, but the women still work.'

'We are good at that,' said Valerie.

'My sister can walk again. Andrei is safe, and Mother will soon have her family living with her. What about you, Valerie Marsh?' He turned his head to look at her. 'What do you intend doing with your life?'

'I intend escorting you back to Mavara tomorrow, and remaining there for as long as you, and your family, need me.'

'And then?' he said. 'Will you return to England once the war is over?'

'I don't know,' she said. 'The Nurse-in-Charge thinks it will go on for a long time. So when you no longer need me I will return to Kiev and continue nursing.'

'What if I asked you to stay? Could you spend the rest of your life with a bad-tempered, broken wreck, Valerie Marsh?'

Without a word Valerie leaned over and cupped his face in her hands. Then she brushed her lips gently across his scarred flesh and rested them softly on his mouth.

'I'll stay with you always, Pyotr,' she said, lifting her head. 'I'll be your mistress, or nurse, whatever you want as long as we are together.'

'As my wife,' he said, reaching down beneath the blankets and bringing out the ring with his good hand. 'This is for you, Varinka. At last it will be worn by the one I truly love.'

As she remained speechless, staring at the magnificent Silakov heirloom, he let out a curse.

'I want to hold you close and place this on your finger, but with one hand I am useless, damn it!'

'Hush.' Valerie took the ring from him and slid it onto her finger. 'There, now it is on my hand and I promise you *I* will not be breaking this engagement. But it needs to be made smaller.' She took it off and tried it on her middle finger. 'There, that's better.'

'It will be made smaller the moment we return,' he said. 'And I shall see the priest in Kamenka and arrange our marriage for the first possible day. Come to me, my love, and ease my loneliness.'

As Valerie moved to lie against his good side, she felt his arm go round her and she thought of her father and Mrs Duffy, and how she would enjoy writing to tell them of her forthcoming marriage to a Russian count.

Once the war was over and Pyotr had learnt to accept his changed appearance, they would travel to England as man and wife and he would be introduced to Putney.

Maybe they would also go to Petrograd and

see Grand Duchess Olga again at Tsarskoe Selo? Surely the Empress would forgive Valerie the past, once she had wed the young officer whom the Imperial family had liked so much?

There were so many possibilities, so many hopes for the future, once she became Pyotr's wife and the world had returned to sanity and peace.

We do hope that you have enjoyed reading this large print book.

Did you know that all of our titles are available for purchase?

We publish a wide range of high quality large print books including:
Romances, Mysteries, Classics
General Fiction
Non Fiction and Westerns

Special interest titles available in large print are:
The Little Oxford Dictionary
Music Book
Song Book
Hymn Book
Service Book

Also available from us courtesy of Oxford University Press:
Young Readers' Dictionary
(large print edition)
Young Readers' Thesaurus
(large print edition)

For further information or a free brochure, please contact us at:
Ulverscroft Large Print Books Ltd.,
The Green, Bradgate Road, Anstey,
Leicester, LE7 7FU, England.
Tel: (00 44) 0116 236 4325
Fax: (00 44) 0116 234 0205

Other titles published by Ulverscroft:

HONEY BROWN IS MARRIED

Sara Judge

March 1950: ex-showgirl Honey Brown has married the farmer she adores — August Blake Esq. — and though she pines for the bright lights and glamour of the Windmill Theatre, her new mother-in-law, Doris, is determined to turn Honey into a respectable lady of the manor. To make matters worse, as well as the struggle to meet Doris's exacting standards, Honey feels increasing animosity towards dairy-man Nick. Why does she dislike him, when everyone else seems to find him so agreeable? When enmity between the two turns to disaster, Honey wonders if her life on the farm is really worth fighting for.

MISS DARCY'S PASSION

Wendy Soliman

When Dominic Sanford's parents die in a carriage accident, he is packed off to Scotland to be brought up in his uncle's household. Years later, he returns to his dilapidated estate that borders Pemberley. His father's journals have recently come into his possession, raising questions about his parents' deaths . . . Upon seeing Dominic for the first time at Colonel Fitzwilliam's wedding, Georgiana Darcy feels an immediate attraction. As she assists him in delving deeper into his family's history, they uncover a fiendish web of organised criminality. But Georgiana unwittingly plays a major role in the miscreants' plans — by involving her, Dominic has placed her directly in danger's path . . .

BOOK LOVERS

Linda M. Priestley

Amy moves into her aunt Debbie's house to study and to help her aunt through chemotherapy. The last thing on Amy's mind is romance — she's been hurt before — but when a charming stranger wanders into the house, mistaking it for its former incarnation as a second-hand book shop, Debbie is irresistibly drawn to him, despite her uncertainty as to whether he is a burglar or a genuine book lover. To complicate matters, Uncle Bernard, Debbie's dubious ex, suddenly appears on the scene, inveigling his way into the household and back into Debbie's heart. What are Bernard's real motives, and can Amy really trust the new object of her affections?

HANNAH'S WAR

Fenella J. Miller

World War II brings divided loyalties and tough decisions for Hannah Austen-Bagshaw. Her privileged background can't stop her falling in love with working-class pilot Jack — but Hannah has a secret. Torn between her duty and her humanity, she is sheltering a young German pilot, all the while knowing she risks being arrested as a traitor. Hannah's worst fears are realised when Jack finds out what she has done and their love begins to unravel. Will her betrayal be too much for Jack to forgive?